Evil can lurk in the most innocent of young, wounded hearts.

Detectives Tara Woods and Matt Dobbs signed in at the murder scene, both sleep deprived.

The weekend night was muggy. A summer downpour was forecasted for some time before daylight. Clouds covered the moon and stars. The police cars' blue strobe lights danced with an eerie ballet across their faces and the large, three-story, red brick home in front of them.

Tara rubbed the goose bumps from her arms and counted four police cars called to the scene. The Medical Examiner's van sat against the curb in front of the house. Behind it was the forensic van.

Someone thought it was the perfect night for a double homicide.

Jeri Lynn Stone lives in a small Arkansas town with her husband. They own a small cattle farm and she works at a large manufacturing plant in the Quality Assurance Department as an ISO Internal Auditor and Quality Assurance. Her and her husband love to camp and fish. They live in the center of four beautiful lakes and each are within twenty-five miles from home. They love going to antique car shows, gardening and Mother Nature. She has enjoyed writing novels, from historical to chicklit to mystery for about twelve years, now. She's currently working on the third novel in her Detective Mystery "Tara" series.

BOOKS BY JERI LYNN STONE
'TARA' DETECTIVE SERIES
TAUNTING TARA

TEACHING TARA

COMING NEXT
TANGLE WITH TARA

TEACHING TARA

ACKNOWLEDGEMENT

I would like to thank my wonderful husband, my family, my husband's family, friends, and the wonderful writers' communities for the loving support they've given me all of these years. I'm very grateful and honored to have everyone in my life.

I would also like to thank my terrific critique partners. They keep me on the straight and narrow path in my writing career.

And, to my fans. You are the greatest. I appreciate you all.

Thank you,
Jeri Lynn Stone

Jeri Lynn Stone

~

TEACHING TARA

~

2 NOVEL IN THE "TARA" SERIES

CHAPTER ONE

Evil can lurk in the most innocent of young, wounded hearts.

In the darkened foyer, Bob Chambers prepared to punch in his home security code. Sensing a malicious presence next to him, his hand stilled. Before he could shout a warning to his wife behind him, he felt a sharp object plunge into his stomach. A piercing pain stunned him. The air exhaled from his lungs.

He yelled out in fear and struggled as hard as his eighty–five year old feeble body could manage.

He had to protect his wife of sixty years. Had to.

The struggle earned him a hard blow to the head. He heard his beloved Edna scream as his knees hit the marbled floor, the object ripping through his chest. Moaning, he tried to rise.

That's when he saw through the bloody haze another masked assailant stab his wife with repeated thrusts. He screamed and cried out as she fell to the floor, the blood draining from her limp body. "Nooooooo. Edna? Please, not my wife. Please God. Please God. No." He prayed.

The knife entered his body, over and over.

Knowing his life was soon over, his hand reached out for his love, one last time.

CHAPTER TWO

Detectives Tara Woods and Matt Dobbs signed in at the murder scene, both sleep deprived from their last case they'd recently solved and closed.

The weekend night was muggy hot. A summer downpour was forecasted for some time before daylight. Clouds covered the quarter moon and stars. The police cars' blue strobe lights danced with an eerie ballet across their faces and illuminated the large, three-story, red brick home in front of them.

Someone thought it was the perfect night for a double homicide.

Tara rubbed the sweat from her hands onto her blue jeans and counted four police cars called to the scene. The Medical Examiner's van sat against the curb in front of the house. Behind it was the forensic van.

Tara and Dobbs pulled out their protective gloves and boots from their bags and put them on before entering through the front door.

"What do we have, Ben?" Tara asked the medical examiner squatted beside the male victim. She thought the examiner looked a lot like the handsome Russell Crowe, her favorite actor. She rubbed her eyes and covered a yawn as she looked around the scene.

Ben Marks glanced up as they drew near and nodded his head in a greeting. "Tara. Dobbs. I see you two drew the short end of the stick and won the case. We have a husband and wife, both I would say in their mid-eighties stabbed multiple times. The wounds are consistent to the depth of a long-bladed pocket knife."

Dobbs glanced up. "A stiletto switchblade, maybe? Gang related?"

"From the slices made, that's the weapon I would put my money on. Autopsy may change my mind, but I doubt it. As far as gang related, that's your expertise." Ben continued. "The blood is confined to the front entrance of the home. By the bruising on the man's face and a deep gash on the back of his head, he struggled with the killer before being overpowered. The woman shielded her face and body. Her arms, hands and shoulders had several deep cuts across them from the effort. The blade was plunged into her stomach four times and twice into her lung area. She collapsed to the floor, gone in an instant. I would put their deaths around ten or ten-thirty this evening. I'll pin it down to more of an exact time and cause when I do the autopsy."

"Thanks, Ben. That's around the time the security company called it in." Careful to stay away from the evidence, Tara stuck her gloved thumbs into her jeans front pockets and circled the two bodies lying on the tiled floor.

The elderly man, gray-haired and close to Dobb's height and build of 6' 2" and a hundred and eighty pounds lay on his side. His hand reached toward his wife as if to protect her. Drying blood pooled around him.

The woman, who looked a little smaller than Tara's 5' 6" and one hundred and twenty-five pounds lay a few feet him in a bloody, crumbled heap. A few hairpins littered the floor causing her gray hair to escape the stylish bun and partially cover her face. Parts or her blue gown was now red.

Both victims wearing evening clothes looked to be returning home from a night out. It was evident from their location and the blood splatter on the wall and floor that as soon as they both entered the elegant, multi-million dollar home, they were murdered.

Tara nodded to the officer working the case. "Jackson, what have you found?"

Officer Jackson, a twenty-five year veteran pulled his pants up and over his large belly before he walked over to Tara and Dobbs with his notebook in hand. "I would say, from where the male victim lay, he entered first and the wife came in behind him. They were attacked from the front, so the killers were already inside. There were two killers. Two weapons. Each killed their own victim. She would've either helped her husband to fight his assailant or ran back out the door for help if there were only one. She did neither. No struggle marks on her body, only defensive. But, there are on his. Unless, she was involved and they turned on her after killing the old man."

Dobbs agreed. "Possible. Won't rule it out." His brows gathered as he studied the couple. "Tell me something. I don't know much about it, but what woman would dress for a party in a long, expensive looking designer gown and not adorn themselves with jewelry? I've never met one, anyway."

Tara glanced down and studied the couple and nodded in thought. "You're right. Not even a wedding ring, but you can tell by the indent on her finger she wore one. Robbery gone bad?"

"Maybe." Dobbs pointed at the controls on the wall. "State of the art security system with motion sensors. Best money can buy and the killers still got inside without sending an alert. The alarm sounded after the couple entered and they were murdered before they could punch in the code to reset it. Which means, the robbers turned it off before they entered and turned it back on as they were leaving to not raise suspicion. The couple must have arrived home earlier than expected and surprised them as they were leaving."

"Or, the female vic let them in."

Dobbs nodded with hesitancy. "Or, she let them in."

"But, you don't think so."

"I don't know. It's looking more like a robbery to me." Dobbs started toward the living area. "Let's see if we can find out what else is missing besides the jewelry."

Tara followed and saw one of the police officers making notes on the destroyed room. It looked like a tornado had come through, she thought. A long, soft blue, cloth-covered sofa and a matching chair were turned over on their backs. A broken Tiffany lamp lay on the carpet. A small round table sitting between the sofa and the chair lay on its side. A pair of reading glasses, books and magazines were lying beside the table.

Nothing else was left in the room. The walls and mantles were bare. No paintings. No knick knacks or any type of valuables were lying around. On one wall a safe stood open. On closer inspection, Tara saw it was empty, which with everything else proved Dobbs' theory of a possible robbery.

Tara approached the rookie deputy. "Banks, what do you have?"

Banks glanced up from his notes and greeted them with a youthful, shy smile. "Tara. Dobbs. The victims are Boyd and Edna Chambers."

"As in Senator Chambers parents?" Dobbs asked.

Banks nodded. "Yep."

Tara swore and rubbed her neck. "I thought they looked familiar. This isn't going to be good. All hell is going to break loose when the Senator gets the news."

"Guess we need to warn Chief Haynes." Dobbs pulled out his cell and began punching in the numbers.

"Tell him you're taking lead in this investigation." Tara said.

"Like hell I am. They don't call the Senator "Ball Buster" Chambers for nothing."

CHAPTER THREE

A little after midnight, Teach stared at his reflection in the mirror as he loosened his silk tie, blue to match his eyes. He was pleased with his appearance. The Italian suit he wore for the party tonight cost him a small fortune, but well worth the price. He'd get his money back on the clothing.

At twenty-five, his six foot stature, street toned body, blonde hair, strong chiseled chin, sensuous smile and charming ways added up to what women lusted after and men envied. And, they let him know it.

He never let them see the evil lurking inside him.

He no longer resembled the scrawny thirteen year old who bore the numerous scars from the belt lashings he'd endured from his father. Or, the back handed slaps his drunken mother had 'lovingly' dealt him.

All he could remember from his earlier years is that they'd moved around at least every two or three months. It depended on how long it took before someone noticed the bruises on him. Then, they would flee to another town, another school.

One night when his father was angry at the world and at his meanest and his mother was passed out drunk on the sagging couch, he'd had enough. He'd wiped the blood off his face from another beating, grabbed the sharpest kitchen knife and stabbed his father over and over, maybe thirty times or more while he was sleeping. Then, he poured a bottle of cheap whiskey over his mother's prone drunken body. He'd felt the thrill as the match flared to life and his mother went up in flames. He always knew the liquor would kill her one day, he thought.

He'd watched her burn and prayed she went straight to hell before the sound of sirens in the distance had him stuffing his parent's money into his pocket and running out the back door. Carl Mason was thirteen years old.

Years later, he'd bought false identification and changed his name. He never knew if anyone looked for him after the fire. He figured they did, but it didn't matter. He was too smart to let them find him.

By the time he was fifteen he'd lived off the streets of New York for two years. At seventeen, he knew every dirty trick to survive in a city crawling with thieves, gangs, drug dealers and murderers. At twenty he was a master thief and he'd killed whomever got in his way. At twenty-five he was a millionaire in his own right. He'd stolen his way to the top of his game.

Street smarts came easy to him. No one had bested him. And, it pleased him to take four more runaway juvenile delinquents with police records under his wing and teach them the skills they needed to be part of his team.

He'd told everyone he met that he was a commercial real estate mogul and dressed the part. He'd opened an office and hired four realtors to make it authentic. Before he knew it, everyone believed him.

It was one of his best cons, yet.

He owned a luxurious penthouse, a Ferrari and a Maserati. And, he was invited to every elite party given by the richest and most powerful people in New York.

Yet, it wasn't enough.

He was still that little beaten boy in his mind and heart.

And to this day he still blamed his mother. He blamed her for not taking up for him with his father when he abused him. He blamed her for allowing his father to beat her down to a drunken nothing. He blamed her for not loving him enough. But, he showed her and hoped she rotted in hell.

His lips now turned down into a frown as he turned away from his reflection. He had a secret. One that only four others knew. His young protégés.

Oh, and the robbed victims who had left the party too early tonight.

But, thanks to his student's failure to follow his orders, the victims weren't talking.

CHAPTER FOUR

At 5 a.m., the city's street sweepers were loaded up and gone, the streets clean for only a short while. The smell of fresh coffee, food and urine filled Tara's nostrils from an occasional breeze blowing throughout the city.

Bars were closed tight. Drunks slept the warm night off in dank alley ways and dark doorways. Even the prostitutes, drug sellers, thieves and rats had bedded down until the early evening. In the town that never sleeps, New York City was waiting for the next shift to begin.

Except for the many dedicated officers and detectives whose shifts seems to never end, Tara thought.

Tara and Dobbs left his car on the street and they made their way into their precinct. Reaching her office, Tara lowered her aching body into her chair and opened her desk drawer to pull out a bottle of aspirin.

It had been less than twenty-four hours before when her and Dobbs had solved their latest case. No sooner had they turned in their report on that serial murder case to Chief Haynes when they were called in on this one. She was emotionally and physically exhausted. Pushed to her limit. But, this new case was an improvement over sitting in her apartment and wallowing in self-pity and regrets.

She was better at kicking ass.

Dobbs entered her office carrying two mugs of strong coffee and a box of fresh donuts from a bakery down the street. He placed them on her desk and sat down. Knowing Dobbs, he'd bought enough donuts for the whole unit.

Tara was starving and reached for two. She took a bite out of one filled with cream cheese and moaned, rolling her eyes in ecstasy. Calories, be damned. She'd work them off later today at the gym. If she had time to make it to the gym.

Wiping the yummy crumbs off her mouth with her tongue and napkin, her mind still worked on the case. She asked, "What are the chances these robbers will fence the goods locally?"

"Zilch to none. This wasn't an act of a petty thug wanting a little extra cash in his pocket. We could be talking about organized crime with fingers reaching far and wide. If so, if the items aren't out of the country by now, they soon will be."

Dobbs licked the chocolate cream from his lips and continued. "Which means the bastard snakes will slither back into their holes until the next time. I have Melinda checking on all the recent large scale robberies around New York."

"Sounds good." Melinda Cass was their goddess of computer research. If there was a connection between the robberies, she'd find it. "We don't know if we're dealing with organize, but this isn't the robber's first rodeo. They knew exactly what they were doing and they knew when the Chambers wouldn't be home. We need to talk to Senator Chambers this morning to get a better idea of his parents' routine."

Dobb's reached for another donut, bit into it and settled back in the chair with his feet propped on her desk. "They've been watching the Chambers for a while. Either the older couple goes to a party every Saturday night or the robbers were tipped off that they would be gone for a few hours."

"But, the thieves weren't tipped off they were coming home early. Which may throw my pro theory completely off base. That sounds like a huge rookie mistake to me. A pro would've had a lookout giving them plenty of time to exit before the Chambers' drove down their long driveway, parked and made their way inside. The robbers already had their loot loaded up. All they had to do was drive off and be scott free. Hell, this is New York. Minutes later, they would've pulled into a garage they owned and had their vehicle stripped, repainted and a different license plate put on it. They knew they couldn't be identified. Why stick around and kill the old couple?"

"For the sport, maybe? An adrenaline rush? Who knows?"

Tara wiped the sticky crumbs off her hands, took a sip of her cooling coffee and stood. She stretched and yawned. "Well, let's see what kind of rush we can give them by sending their sleazy butts to the pen for life."

* * *

At 8:00 a.m., cars were already lined up in front of Senator Chambers' massive, colonial home. People were walking in and out after bringing food and offering their condolences. Local broadcasting stations were setting up their equipment on the large, landscaped front lawn.

Bad news traveled fast.

Tara and Dobbs knocked on the Senator's front door and then they both stepped inside as someone was leaving. Tara looked around the spacious foyer and followed the sound of voices leading them to a living area.

She glanced around watching the large number of guests. She studied each one individually. One or more in this room could possibly be the killer or killers returning to gloat, to pat themselves on the back for a job well done.

Senator Chambers and his wife, Gloria with their son Justin dominated the center of the elegant room with a group of sympathizers surrounding them. The wife seemed to keep herself fit, but the Senator sported a body with a larger frame and the beginning of graying hair. Both were well-groomed for the public eye.

But, this morning they looked much older than their sixty plus years from the grief of recently losing loved ones. Weariness clouded their usual smiles that she remembered. Tara sympathized. She knew what it was like to have your parents murdered. It was hell to live through and never went away.

Tara and Dobbs made their way toward the couple and their son. Tara greeted Mrs. Chambers and Justin. She turned to the Senator and softened her words. "Senator Chambers, we're so sorry for your loss."

The Senator nodded. "Thank you, Detective. I understand you two are on the case. I'm glad. I have the upmost confidence in the two of you."

"Yes Sir and thank you. We'll do our best. I know this is not the best time, but may we have a few minutes of your time, Senator? We have a few questions we need to ask."

"Certainly. But first, let me quickly introduce you to a few friends. This is Larry and Kay Brightons and this young guy is Chase Masters."

Tara and Dobbs greeted a well-dressed younger man and an older, obviously polished man with his lovely wife on his arm. They spoke for a moment before the three moved off to allow the Senator a chance to talk to the detectives.

Tara shook off her uneasiness. The look in the youngest guest's eyes gave her the creeps. It was like looking into the emotionless eyes of a cold-blooded murderer. She'd seen plenty in her career. But, that didn't mean one of the Senator's guest was actually a murderer. Still, Tara memorized the guest's name. She would check his credentials out later. As well as everyone else who was there.

The Senator turned to his wife. "Gloria, I'll only be a few minutes. Can you send us coffee into my office, please?"

Gloria squeezed his hand and offered a weak smile. "Take your time. Detectives, thank you. We want to help you in any way to catch whoever did this to Mama and Papa Chambers."

"Thank you, Mrs. Chambers. We won't keep him long."

The Senator spoke to his guests for a short moment and excused himself before leading Tara and Dobbs to his private home office. Offering them a seat, he rounded his desk and sat.

A soft knock sounded and a young housekeeper entered carrying a tray with their coffee. After serving everyone she left them alone.

Shaking off his obvious exhaustion, the Senator leaned forward, his normal brusqueness emerging. "First and foremost, I want you to catch the bastard who did this to my parents. I don't care what you do. Do whatever you have to do to get it done. Understand?"

Tara and Dobbs nodded. "Yes, Sir."

Dobbs added, "We'll bring justice to your parents, Sir. Within the means of the law, of course."

The Senator studied them for a moment as if struggling with Dobbs' last sentence. He finally nodded in agreement. "Good. That's what I want to hear. What do you need to know from me?"

"We need to know more about your parent's activities last night. Where did they go for the evening?" Tara asked.

"The Brightons that we were just talking to are good friends of ours. Larry and Kay Brightons hosted a small party in the honor of one of their guest son's upcoming marriage. They've been friends with Mom and Dad for years. I talked to my mother earlier yesterday evening and she said Dad wasn't feeling well, but he insisted he felt well enough to go. He had a heart attack about a year ago and at his age he hadn't fully bounced back from the surgery. I imagine that's why they left early."

Tara wrote the names down. "We'll question the Brightons and get a guest list from them. Senator, I have to ask, did your parents have any enemies, someone with a grudge against one or both?"

"Hell, no. Everyone they knew, in business and in their personal lives loved them. They were invited to every social get-together given within their circle of friends. They've hosted large gatherings in their home over the years, as well. No, I can't believe it was anything other than a robbery gone bad. If my parents had stayed maybe ten minutes longer at the party, they would still be alive. Just ten minutes." The Senator rubbed his teary eyes and sat back. His hand shook.

Even a hard-boiled Senator of the United States can be brought to his knees over a senseless murder of his parents. Tara closed her notepad and sat her coffee cup on the desk. "We'll leave you alone now, Sir. We'll find who did this and make them pay."

The Senator looked up. "Thank you. I just pray to God that you find them before they kill again."

"Me too, Sir."

CHAPTER FIVE

The Teacher slammed his student against the wall and held him there with a tight fist clenched to the boy's t-shirt, his eyes crystal cold. "You stupid bastard." He glanced toward the other boy standing in the doorway. They'd finally come home to accept their punishment.

"I should kill you both." He let go of the t-shirt and slammed his fist into the boy's abdomen. The boy slid to the floor and earned a kick to the ribs, not hard enough to break them, but to bruise. He didn't want him out of commission.

The next test was coming up.

BoneZ, his new surveillance tech laid there without a whimper. The dark-skinned, eighteen-year-old boy from Atlanta was still green after a month's training. But, he was good. He knew his way around security systems, wires and trackers. His specialty was using Google Earth to study the aerial photos of their intended victim's homes to determine the best points of entry. With a little more training he would no longer be good. He'd be the best. Or, he'd be dead. His option.

The Teacher glanced back toward the doorway. "Get the hell in here."

Gator, a tall, handsome Louisiana Cajun with black hair and large, muscled biceps stepped into the room. Raised in the swamps, the quiet sixteen-year-old wasn't scared of anything. When his mother, his only surviving relative died from a fever when he was fourteen, he took off and grabbed the first bus out of there. When the Teacher found him he was living off the streets, eating out of garbage cans and fighting for his survival. Still, to him it was a hell of a lot better than foster care.

Gator was fast on his feet and had the ability to empty a room of its valuables within a few short minutes. If it weren't for his trigger temper, he would've been one of his best students. Given time, the temper could be controlled. And, would be.

The Teacher's knee slammed into the boy's genitals sending him to his knees. Turning away from him, he glanced around the luxurious room with a scowl and eyed the other two boys.

Cruiser, the third member of his team sat on the leather recliner with his legs dangling over the chair arm. With a purple Mohawk, a silver looped earring dangling from one ear and a slight gap between his teeth he looked more like a sixteen year old hard rocker, instead of a once penniless, habitual runaway who'd lived off the streets for the past two years. The boy had a dark edginess about him and that combined with his specialty skills allowed him to become chosen as part of his team.

Cruiser had the unique talent to break into anything that was locked. Cars, homes, vaults or computers. It didn't matter. If the Teach wanted in, Cruiser made it happen. He was also their look out and get-away apprentice.

His oldest student, Striker, who got his name from once using a cats head as a baseball was earning his masters in the art of thievery. He was his best pupil and second in command.

Striker had studied under him for three years and was still in training. He would be the first to graduate. He was seventeen, a skinny white boy with long black hair and wild eyes darting around, watching and learning. He'd been living off the streets as a runaway for four years.

According to the boy, he'd never looked back to his rich life style and the painful neglect. Now, he leaned against the wall watching the boys' punishment, a slight, arrogant grin turning up his lip. He'd been in their shoes, once. Only once. You learn fast in this game.

The Teacher turned to his four hand-picked students. "You disobeyed me. This was supposed to be a clean job. You failed."

Gator stood, still leaning over at the waist and breathing through his clenched teeth. His Cajun accent was enhanced from the pain. "You can't blame us for this, Teach. Man, it's not our fault we temporarily lost the phone signal and didn't get your message they were leaving the party early. They walked in as we were leaving. What were me and BoneZ supposed to do? They saw our faces."

The Teacher clenched and unclenched his fists gaining control of his temper. He pointed a finger at Striker and with a calmer, controlled classroom voice, he asked, "Can you tell these students what they were supposed to've done?"

Striker looked at his clean nails in a bored manner and with a quiet monotone voice, he answered. "You idiots were taught this in the first week of training. You should know this shit. You never, ever take off your masks or gloves while on the job. You do not panic and make stupid ass mistakes like last night. Never draw a weapon unless you have no other option. Keep a clear head at all times. Within a split second you may have to make life-altering decisions. Make damn sure it's the right one."

The Teach nodded his approval. "Good. Good. Thank you, Striker. Boys, I think the most important lessons you need to take away from this unforgivable mistake is that you can be replaced. Each and every one of you. And, you know I can't allow my secrets to be known. I have too much at stake. I've taken you boys into my home and I'm spending my valuable time and money to teach you all of the life skills you will ever need to survive off the streets."

He clapped his hands together and ended his speech. "So my fellow students, to fail my class, you die. Bottom line. You knew and agreed on my grading system when you signed on. But, when you graduate and earn my trust you'll have more money than you can ever spend in a life time. That's your reward. Understand?" He glared at each one until they nodded in agreement.

"So Teach, what about the detectives who'll be nosing around asking questions? What are you going to do about them?" Striker asked.

"Not a damn thing. For now." He grinned and scoffed. "Hell, I met the two of them face to face at the Senator's home this morning. As far as they know, I'm a good friend of the family and when they ask, I'll have the perfect alibi. I have several witnesses to state I left the party two hours after the old couple was murdered. And, we've been careful to not let anyone see any of you coming or going. You no longer exist to the outside world. Nothing to worry about, boys."

He rubbed his chin and kept the rest of his thoughts to himself. He'd seen the two detectives on the recent news. They cracked three murder cases in the past year. They were good.

Especially the female. What was her name? Oh yeah, Detective Tara Woods. She had looked him straight in the eyes at the Senator's house and had stepped back as if she'd smelled something foul before turning her back on him to speak to the Senator's wife. Stupid woman. Her actions had pissed him off royally. She looked at him like the low-life he used to be before he'd made something of himself. He was as good or better than her, both in his life and career, he seethed. She was not much better than his mother.

He'd teach her.

CHAPTER SIX

After a few hours of stolen sleep and a quick shower at their separate apartments, Tara and Dobbs met back up at headquarters a little after four Sunday evening. Down to a minimal weekend crew, the building was quieter than the usual chaos going on during the week. But, drug heads, drunks and street walkers were still being led through to be processed.

Wearing blue jeans and an old T-shirt with a design proclaiming her dislike of spiders, rats and exercise, Tara sat at her desk with her pen tapping against the sheets of paper provided by the Senator's housekeeper.

The long list contained the names of all the sympathizers who showed up at the Senator's home this morning. Tara recognized several from seeing their pictures in the newspaper social page. The others, she would need to find out more about them. One of them could very well be the murderer gloating in their faces.

She remembered one younger man who'd sent off bad vibes in her gut. She'd figured it was the cop in her that had her looking closer into his eyes with mistrust, because the woman in her found him very attractive.

But, those eyes. Strange. He might not be the person they were looking for. Probably not. But, she'd have him checked out. He was hiding something, she knew. She'd seen a similar coldness in those eyes as she had in a convicted murderer. He was no innocent and he couldn't hide it from her with that gorgeous smile. She'd been immune to the smile and to him.

She had Jake, her live-in boyfriend in her life, now. And, he was all she wanted or needed even when he was out of town on business for his art gallery, like this weekend. She'd missed his kisses this morning.

Tara sighed and forced her mind back on the case.

Dobbs sat across from her in his casual fitting jeans and muscled short sleeve shirt reading through the short list of guests who had been at Larry and Kay Brightons' get-together Saturday night. The Brightons also gave an approximate time when each guest had arrived and left their home.

Comparing the two lists to see who attended both would give them a good starting place in the investigation.

Dobbs called off the names on his party list and Tara checked them off on hers. Other than the two victims, all of the other fifteen party-goers had shown up at the Senator's home the next day. Unfortunately, according to the Brightons they had all left the party at least a couple of hours or longer after the murders took place.

Tara flipped her pen onto the desk and sat back. Rubbing her stiff neck, she said, "I still want to send some officers out to talk to these people. It's going to be time consuming, but I'd rather eliminate than to overlook someone."

"I agree. I'll call Chief Haynes and ask for overtime for a couple of officers and we can go from there."

Tara nodded. "In the meantime, let's pay Melinda a visit to see if any other similar robberies were reported."

Taking the elevator to the third floor, Tara and Dobbs walked to Melinda Cass's office. They found the department's computer expert, a dark haired, slender girl in her mid-twenties. She was wearing low riding blue jeans and a dark red t-shirt topping her midriff and moving with a fluid be-bopping way between three computers sitting on a horseshoe shaped table.

A printer on one corner spit out pages of information as she typed on one of the computer. She glanced up and a wide grin appeared. "Hey, my Sweets. Just in time." She grabbed the stack of sheets off the printer and gave Dobbs a saucy wink before she handed the information to him.

"A couple of drinks and a little foreplay later will be payment enough for my hard work on a Sunday evening."

Dobbs grinned. "You're such a tease. If I wasn't so scared of your husband, I'd take you up on it."

Tara grinned. The running friendly flirtation between Melinda and Dobbs would never go anywhere. Undercover officer Blake Cass, Melinda's husband of two years was one of Tara's, Jake's and Dobbs' good friends. Dobbs had been the best man at their wedding and they all met when they could for a pizza and beer. "Don't worry Dobbs. She's not going to trade in her young hunk of a husband for you. It would be like trading in a new Ferrari for an antique Volkswagen."

Dobbs' brow rose. "Thanks a lot."

Tara grinned. "Anytime. Melinda, what do you have for us?"

Melinda's teasing smile turned serious as she turned back to her computer and pulled up a screen. "Those sheets I gave you are printouts of all the home robberies within a hundred mile radius and within a six month period. Thirty five in all. But, I've narrowed it down to twelve high dollar hits." She pulled up a map with pinpoints showing the locations of the twelve homes. They were all within twenty five miles of each other.

Tara studied the map. "Who's working these cases?"

Melinda clicked a couple of keys. "Looks like it's Manhattan's Robbery Detective Adam Landers."

"Thanks, Melinda. Lose the husband and I'll pay up." Dobbs grabbed her in a bear hug.

Melinda snorted and pushed at his chest. "Yeah, right. Get the hell out of here so I can go and spend the rest of my day off with my husband...my Ferrari."

Tara laughed out loud. "We're out of here. Dobbs' grab your crushed ego and let's see if we can find Landers at home."

* * *

An hour later, Tara and Dobbs sat in Detective Landers living room where he'd been relaxing in his sweats, drinking a cold beer and watching the last few laps of a NASCAR race on TV. He lowered the volume.

After twenty years as a Robbery Detective for the NYPD, the veteran officer was reaching retirement age. His weathered face and gray hair showed the hard years along with the keen intelligence in his dark blue eyes. "What can I do for you, Detectives?"

Dobbs answered. "I understand you're working the recent break-ins, plus the one from last night that is part of our homicide investigation. We believe a few are connected, somehow. What can you tell us about these twelve?" Dobbs handed him the sheets Melinda had provided.

Landers pulled at his chin as he studied the readout. "Yeah, these are mine. I left the last victims home about an hour, ago. Took me a little fishing trip and didn't get back until this morning. Got the full report, though."

He tapped the sheets in his hand. "I see where you're going with this questioning, because I've come to the same conclusion. I'd bet my last dollar every one of these robberies were done by the same group. Other than no murder took place in the other twelve robberies, the MO's the same. The security system was turned off and then back on when they left the residence. No prints found. High dollar merchandise was stolen. They even found hidden items which tells me they knew how long they had to look for the items or knew where to find them. Plus, have time to empty the house of valuables. It wasn't a rush in and rush out job. They knew exactly what they were doing and how much time they had to do it in."

Tara leaned forward. "Inside job?"

Landers shrugged. "It's possible one of the victim's staff took on other jobs around the area. They would know the layout and security of the homes. But, believe me, the staff from each home were all checked out. We're not talking about one thief breaking in at will. It would take more than one to carry the heavy items out and to empty that many rooms in a short time, one or two lookouts, the driver. Could be more. I'm looking for four or five, at the least. The merchandise is getting fenced somehow. We haven't been able to find their exact method of selling, but we haven't seen any of the merchandise show up local. But, it's understandable. They've got fingers reaching far and wide."

"Organized?" Dobbs asked.

"I haven't thrown out the possibility it's part of an organized crime. We're watching them, now. The Bureau has four of their guys infiltrated inside two of the most notorious groups. But, nothing is leading us to believe it's them. I'm not even getting any street chatter about the robberies. None of my informants have heard anything. That's unusual and frustrating as hell."

Knowing they had gotten all they could out of the Detective, Tara stood to leave and offered her hand to shake. "Detective, we appreciate your time and sorry that we've made you miss the ending of your race. Will you keep us posted on anything you find? We'll do the same on our end."

"Oh, no problem. I'm recording the race. Most of the time, I fall asleep before the ending, anyway. Detectives, I wish I knew more to tell you, but I'll be happy to work with you on this latest murder and robbery. It's got me scratching my head in exasperation, I tell you."

With a grim smile, Dobbs leaned over to shake the detective's hand. "We know the feeling, Sir."

CHAPTER SEVEN

Monday morning after a late night of interviewing the Chambers neighbors with no luck and a few hours of needed sleep Tara and Dobbs were back at their desks. While Dobbs worked with the Chambers' insurance company to get copies of the items they had insured e-copied to them, Tara read the police officer's report on the couple.

It didn't tell her any more than what they already knew. No official determined death, but noted multiple stab wounds into vital organs and loss of blood. Also noted was the bare walls and open safe indicating the couple had been robbed before or after the murder. The forensic report was still out on any DNA or prints, but no forced entry was found at the scene.

Left out of the detailed report, but Tara knew the couple had long minutes of suffering before they succumbed to death a few precious minutes before the police and paramedics arrived.

With an effort to control her emotions, she pushed back the old dark memories of the knife blade going into her eight year old body. Over and over. She'd been lucky enough to survive the attack. The Chambers hadn't.

With a trembling hand, she dropped the report onto her desk and stood. Walking toward the small window overlooking the bleak parking lot with cruisers and personal vehicles filling the spaces, she pinched her bottom lip and turned her thoughts back to the murder.

She wasn't tech savvy, she left that up to Dobbs and Melinda. But, even she knew about the Google Earth map. She'd once Googled her own apartment and watched her boyfriend, Jake drive away in his black BMW. She remembered the uneasiness she'd felt at the time. Anyone could spy on her as she came and went from her apartment.

All it took was a high speed internet connection on their phone, computer or tablet and an address for someone to watch the Chambers' home to know if they were there or not. It was possible they'd been watching the elderly couple's home for weeks, even months to learn their habits. The robbery was a big hit, worth thousands of dollars, worth the invested time spent.

Tara wondered if it was possible to track down individuals doing the Google Earth map search by location. She'd ask Dobbs. But, she had a feeling if it was easy enough to be tracked, it would be easy enough to block anyone trying to put a track on their phones or computers. Even though technology changed daily, there's always someone who tries to outsmart the system. She knew when obtaining any digital evidence from a computer or phone, it was necessary to have proper legal authority in order to perform a forensics investigation. The fourth amendment ruled.

It was something to consider.

Tara walked over to her new constructed crime board stationed against the back wall. She'd placed a picture of the two victims in the center of the white board with the son, Senator Chambers and his wife on one side. They'd been at a charity function that Saturday night. Plenty of witnesses, including the cop who arrived at the party to give them the bad news. He'd stated the younger Chambers and his wife were still there when the murder of his parents took place. And, according to the other charity guests at their table, the Chambers had never left.

Then, the pictures of the party hosts, husband and wife Larry and Kay Brightons with their fifteen guests went up next. Other than the murderers, the party guests were the last to see the couple alive. She wanted to talk to them, again. Maybe they remembered something further.

Tara rubbed her hands over her face and blew out a frustrated breath. Dammit. Why didn't the older couple stay at the party ten minutes longer as Senator Chambers stated? Just ten minutes and it would've been the Robbery Investigation Department's problem. Not Homicide.

She jerked from her thoughts as Dobbs walked into her office. "What did you find?"

Dobbs waved a folder in the air before sitting across from her. He pushed the file toward her. "Pictures and serial numbers. The older Chambers were diligent in keeping everything documented and insured."

Tara felt a sizzle of excitement as she opened the file. This information could be crucial in their investigation. She flipped through the pictures and whistled over the prices placed on the art and objects they had insured.

Having a boyfriend who owned an art gallery helped her to recognize some of the artists listed. But, not all. She would run these by the gallery later to see what Jake could tell her about them. He would know who collected this type of art.

"Man, if I just owned one of these paintings I could quit and live in comfort for the rest of my life after I sold it. Where did they get all of their money?" Tara asked.

Dobbs leaned back in his chair. "The old-fashioned way. They inherited it. Ever hear of the Charlston Chablis?"

"Of course. I have a couple of bottles in my cabinet. One of my favorites. Why?"

"Edna Charlston Chambers' family owns the wine company. She is ... was a silent partner of three. Her two brothers Mark and Allen Charlston run the mega million company."

"Hmmm. Let's check out the brothers in case one-third of a mega million isn't enough to tide them over. Maybe, they needed the sister's, too."

"Possible, but they live in California. It would be easy enough to find out if one or both left town for a few days. Now, the deceased Mr. Chambers Sr., as you know was a retired Senator and recently a lawyer in his family's law firm, Chambers and Chambers. His father started the firm back in the late 1800's. Chambers' son, Senator Chambers Jr. left his father's lawyers office and ran for Senate two years, ago and won. Now, the recent Senator's only son, thirty-four year old Justin Chambers III has a law degree and has taken over running the law office with a couple of junior lawyers beneath him. They have a lot of huge cases beneath their belts, celebrity and high-profile murder cases. I would say Justin is doing pretty well with the family law practice."

"No hidden, bitter family members left out of the inheritance?" Tara asked.

"None that I could find. All of the cousins on Mrs. Chambers side inherited equally and on Mr. Chambers side, each generation had only one child, a son who took over the practice when it was their time."

Tara thought about what Dobbs said. No one's family got along this well. But, still that didn't make them murderers. "So, I feel safe to eliminate the family members for now. I'd rather we concentrated solely on the robbery gone bad."

Dobbs nodded. "I agree." He pointed toward the file in her hands. "There were no pictures of the six paintings on file, but they were all heavily insured, as well as the jewelry. Take a look at the chunk of diamonds and jewels on those wedding rings and the other jewelry. They're worth a small fortune."

Tara flipped through the pages and found pictures of the couple's wedding rings inherited from his parents. 18K rose gold antique wedding rings and matching band for him. Mid-Victorian era. Her wedding ring had six rose cut diamonds, four square emeralds and two oval garnets. Insured for $20,000. And, that was only her wedding rings. Everything combined added up to over $500,000.

Tara dropped the file on her desk. "You know what's so sad?"

"What?"

"From what we gathered from the scene and from the family and friends, there was more love than money in that family and with the kind of money these folks have, that's a whole lot of love."

Dobbs nodded. "Sad, isn't it?"

Tara remembered her questions about Google Earth and asked Dobbs what he knew about it. "Can you track views...hits, dings, whatever you want to call it off of Google Earth?"

Dobbs shook his head. "We can find out for sure, but the little I know about it came from a forensic expert who gathered the data off the actual computer or cell they'd confiscated."

"So, you have to examine the actual device they used to Google before the data will show up?"

"I believe so. But, I could be wrong."

"Worth a try to find out. Let's get Melinda working on it."

"I'm on it."

CHAPTER EIGHT

Tara and Dobbs entered Jake's art gallery late Monday evening. Tara called him earlier to let him know they were coming. He'd arrived back from an art show in San Francisco a couple hours before and was busy listing his new finds.

Tara glanced around the room. It wasn't often she had time to visit the gallery, but she enjoyed looking at his latest acquisitions when she could. Jake had worked hard to make it one of the finest galleries in New York and she was proud for him. His gallery supported emerging mid–level and established contemporary artists.

Large, well–lit, white wall showcases about twelve feet long and eight feet tall were situated strategically throughout each room of the four–story building. They featured original paintings, drawings, sculptures, video and photography from artists all over the U.S. .

Jake came out of the back room and greeted them. Since the gallery was open on Mondays,

Tara knew he'd changed out of his traveling clothes, casual and comfortable jeans and t-shirt to a suit and tie. He looked great in them all. Her fingers itched to smooth the white silky material fitting like a second skin across his muscled chest, but knew she had to wait until they were alone. Or even better, to touch his bare chest when he wore nothing at all.

After shaking hands with Dobbs, he turned to Tara. Knowing she was on duty, he settled with a tender squeeze to her hand and a sensual smile and Tara was grateful. She felt uncomfortable with any type of public displays. She would pay back his thoughtfulness later that night if she could get away. They were due some quality time together. She'd bought a new sheer, lacy nightgown while he was gone for the past two days and knew he would love it on her.

Until, he took it off.

As if reading her mind, Jake gave her a promising, sensual wink before leading them into his office. After everyone sat, he asked, "So, what kind of information were you needing?"

"We're looking for several pieces of stolen art and heirloom jewelry from a recent robbery. We're hoping you can help us with leads on the paintings. We're looking into the different ways a thief could fence them," Dobbs told him.

Tara filled him in on the recent robbery/murder. When she finished, Jake nodded.

"I know the paintings you're talking about. The Chambers bought them from me about a year, ago. Good people. They didn't deserve to die like that."

Tara perked up and sat on the edge of the seat. "So, you're familiar with the paintings? Have you heard any whisperings through the art grapevine this morning on where they might be?"

Jake shook his head, his dark hair falling across his eyes. Pushing it back, he said, "No. Nothing, yet. I haven't had time to talk to anyone other than you since I got back into town. Sorry."

"Just a thought. So, how would a thief sell them?"

Jake leaned back in his black, high-back chair and templed his fingertips beneath his chin while he thought. "If it was a high priced art, it would be listed on the FBI's stolen art database by now, as you know. There's no legitimate way to sell a famous painting without the major auction houses finding out about it and then reporting it to the FBI."

"True. But, what about a painting not as well known?" Tara asked.

"The stolen paintings usually end up being traded for about five percent of what it's worth to either a private art collector who has no plan to sell. Or, they trade hands and it goes into the underworld and exchanged for guns and weapons or funds terrorism. But, you are right. We're not talking high priced art, here. This is a lower end painting with not a well-known artist, but they still sell for good money. Here's the thing, if it's not a famous work of art that becomes a high-profile media blast, they could easily enter the legitimate market. There is no legal requirement to have a title provenance document and even those documents can be forged and frequently are."

"I don't think these thieves are very sophisticated in Rembrandts. How would a common thief fence the less well known paintings?" Dobbs asked.

Jake nodded. "I agree. But, I guarantee you they have a plan in place. I would check out pawnshops, flea markets or a low key antique shop. If the store owner knows their business, they'll buy the art for a couple hundred bucks and turn around and sell them to a legitimate art dealer for a thousand or more. Sad thing is that the honest person who ends up buying the painting because they loved it usually ends up being the one who could end up losing their money. Or, end up in trouble with the law for buying stolen goods. "

"True. We've sent out a notice with the descriptions we got from their son and the insurance company to the local galleries and we'll send them out to the other places you mentioned. We appreciate your help, Jake. We'll let you get back to what you were doing." Dobbs told him while rising.

Jake grinned. "Actually, I may have one more thing for you."

Tara leaned forward. "What?"

Jake winked at her and walked out of the office. He came back a moment later with a shiny magazine brochure in his hand. He opened it to a certain page and handed it to Tara. "This is what your stolen paintings look like."

Tara's jaw dropped, a huge grin emerged. She almost broke her own rule and kissed him senseless. But, Dobbs was standing there and she would've never heard the last of it. These photos were priceless. She would make sure they were in the hands of all dealers and in all the law enforcement databases within the hour.

Even though it would be the best exposure to the public, sending them to the media was out for now. They couldn't take the chance the stolen pieces would go so far underground that they were never found.

Tara stole a glance toward Jake. "I owe you."

Jake's gaze was smoldering. "I'll wait up for you tonight."

Dobbs stepped out of the office to give them a moment alone.

Tara stepped closer to Jake. She rested her warm palm against his chest, she couldn't resist the touch. "I'll probably be late."

"Doesn't matter."

* * *

"Annie's missing." Gator rushed into Teach's spacious office lined with bookshelves and valuable collectables and plopped down into a leather guest chair. He sat forward, wringing his shaky hands.

"Are you sure? She might be hiding from you guys trying to get a little peace and quiet." Unconcerned, Teach glanced up from the open screen on the computer sitting on his huge mahogany desk as he spoke.

"Yeah, man. I'm sure. She's gone. Her clothes are missing out of her closet. Even the brown stuffed dog I gave her is gone. Her bedroom window was open, too. She's split, Teach." Gator, the tough kid he was looked like he was about to cry. "I'm real worried, Teach."

Exhausted, Teach sat back and rubbed his face. He believed the boy. He'd been afraid from the very beginning Annie would bolt the first chance she got. Annie was fearful and broken. She was like a beaten dog who cowered and ran before she could be hurt, again. That's the only life she'd known since she'd ran away from home and ended up in a maniac's hands. He sighed and looked at the boy. "Take Cruiser and see if you can find her. Keep me posted."

"Will do, Teach." Gator left the office yelling out Cruiser's name as he ran.

Teach pounded his desk with a fist and stood. He could no longer concentrate on fencing the latest stolen goods or his next job or Detective Woods, right now. His gut clenched. He was worried, too.

Dammit, he couldn't save them all. Thousands of runaway teens ended up in the alleyways of New York each year. Some moved on. Some couldn't handle the life and went back home. Some prostituted themselves in dingy hotel room just to have a place to sleep. And, some died from starvation, overdoses or from severe beatings in those same alleys where he'd fought his way out.

He couldn't save them all. But, he tried to save a few because he'd been in their holey shoes once. His cold heart warmed when he could make the horrific life of a runaway better. He brought them into his home when he could, gave them money for small chores. He fed and clothed them and taught them survival skills until they could fly on their own.

Many learned, but a few returned to the life of prostitution, gangs and addictive drugs on the streets or back into jail. To some, that was safer than returning home.

Like small, blue-eyed Annie.

Gator found her one night next to a dumpster behind a restaurant a couple months back. She'd been beaten almost to deaths door by one of her rough paying clients. She confessed to Teach later that she'd been recruited into prostitution by someone called The Keeper.

As soon as she'd stepped off the Greyhound bus in New York six months, earlier, his goons had taken her. Starving and nowhere else to go, she'd been led into thinking The Keeper would take care of her.

Beaten and starved into submission, she'd learned her lesson the hard way.

Gator picked her up in his arms that night and carried her out of the alley to his car and drove her to Teach's home. Deciding a doctor wasn't needed, Gator and the other students cleaned her up, fed her and put her into a bedroom where they took turns taking care of her with a gentleness Teach didn't know they had.

And, in that short amount of time she'd became their little sister. Someone they could love. They protected and teased her like big brothers do. Teach had grown very fond of the girl, as well.

But, little by little her body had healed and she'd started coming out of her self-protective shell. Little by little, she'd started to smile. To trust.

Until this morning.

Something or someone had scared her enough to make her bolt from the safety of his home without telling her new family.

Someone had gotten past his guard.

Someone had gotten too close.

CHAPTER NINE

Tara buckled her seatbelt and waited until Dobbs pulled out onto the road. She tapped the brochure. "Jake's got me to thinking."

Dobbs checked his side mirror for oncoming traffic before changing lanes. "Oh oh. That's scary."

Tara glanced his way with narrowed brows. "Ha···ha. As I was saying, he's got me to thinking. As he pointed out, those paintings are not Rembrandts. Worth $15,000···,$50,000 tops. That's a big chunk of change for me and you. But, not for the Chambers, the Brightons or the guests at their party that night. They could afford those paintings. So, why steal from a friend?"

"So, you think we should look elsewhere?"

Tara glanced out the side window, her thoughts on the case instead of the heavy traffic around her. "I don't want to take them completely off our list, but yeah, I think we should spend our time looking elsewhere for now. "

"Believe it or not, I agree with you. I think we should concentrate more on the recent robberies Detective Landers mentioned happening over the last two or three months. I think they are a key to our case."

Tara nodded. "Yeah, me too. We can put a couple of uniforms to follow up on the guest list." However, something bothered the hell out of her. She was overlooking something. Something important.

Somehow, the assailants knew when the house would be empty for them to have free reign to rob them. It made sense to her that they planned on having plenty of time to go room to room, getting everything they wanted loaded in their vehicle before the Chambers arrived back home.

Then, the unexpected happened. The Chambers arrived home an hour or two early. It blew the hell out of their plans.

So, they murdered the innocent victims.

Tara rubbed her forehead feeling a nasty headache coming on. She closed her eyes and leaned her head against the cool window for a long moment letting her thoughts run rampant. "We've already established these thieves knew exactly what to target in each room of the home worth stealing. They were quick, precise and knew exactly where to go to retrieve the hidden items without leaving any type of DNA or prints behind. They were professional enough to know with precision ⋯, not guess, but *know* the

Chambers' routine down to the second, knew they were going to that party and would be gone for several hours."

"I hear a but, in there."

Tara nodded her head and continued. "But, you can't tell me these professionals thugs didn't have enough good sense to take into account their victims might arrive back home early. I don't buy it."

Dobbs glanced her way. "I don't either. Something deviated between their other robberies and this one."

"Like me, you're assuming it's the same group of thieves. What if we're wrong? What if Detective Landers is wrong? This could be just a random first time hit by someone who might kill again."

"If so, it's someone else with a fine taste in art and jewels. Detective Landers believes it's the same group responsible for the recent break-ins and I tend to agree. Other than the murder, our case has the same M.O. as his. Everything you just described about our robbery could be said for the ones Landers is investigating." Dobbs turned on his turn signal and merged right with the traffic.

Tara struggled to bring her thoughts to the present. She glanced his way with a frown. "Where are we going?"

"Back to headquarters. We need to see exactly how far these robberies go back and the time frame between the first robbery and the last. Someone is robbing the rich. We need to start there."

* * *

At a quarter to midnight Monday night, Tara climbed the stairs to her apartment. She was exhausted and a light headache still lingered. She and Dobbs had been on a conference call with Detective Landers for the past four hours. He was kind enough to let her and Dobbs review the robbery cases with him.

After going through all of the information in the files of the latest robberies, the three of them agreed that the same group was responsible for both cases. Tuesday morning, the three of them would go over the files on the other robberies and their victims starting around two years ago to compare notes. But, they were all too exhausted to do anything more tonight.

Tara pulled out her key to unlock her door, but before she could insert it, the door opened. Jake stood on the other side with nothing on but a tight pair of unbuttoned jeans and a smile. He held a cold bottle of beer opened and ready for her to drink. She smiled and stepped over the threshold into his arms. He closed the door behind her.

As he promised, he'd waited up for her. And, as she snuggled up to him inhaling his familiar manly, freshly showered scent, she realized her headache and exhaustion were disappearing. Thoughts of her case and any worries vanished as her hands settled on his bare chest.

Between her job and his, they had learned early in their relationship to make the very little precious time they had together worth it. They treasured every moment alone. Jake never complained about her long, dangerous hours spent on the job and she never fussed over his travels when he was gone for several days at a time.

It was part of their lives and they each accepted it.

She'd come close to losing him on the last case when her college friend had become a serial killer against the men whom she'd thought had done her wrong. Her feelings for Jake had grown stronger.

She couldn't call it love as yet, but getting there.

Tara stepped back, reached for the beer and without taking her eyes off of his, she took a swallow and then another. Taking a chance with her heart.

Placing the half empty beer on a nearby coaster, she gave him a wicked look and reached for his hand. Curling her fingers around his, she led him into the bathroom and turned on the shower.

Looking into his burning eyes, she decided the new sheer nightgown would have to wait for another occasion. He wanted her naked and in his arms. Now.

She wasn't complaining.

CHAPTER TEN

No one knows my pain more than the one who sought to destroy my will to survive.

Annie kept her eyes closed. She listened and smelled the familiar pungent smells of rotten vegetables and fruit filling her nostrils. She heard rats, large rats scurrying to the dumpsters for their evening meal outside her prison.

Annie hated rats. These rats. The alley rats.

Annie silenced her whimpers with a fist in her mouth. She was so frightened. But, she couldn't let him see her fears, her pain. Even though her eyes were closed she knew he was near.

The Keeper.

His men had found her hiding place in the dark alley the night before. She knew he'd have someone looking for her, so she'd run from the safe haven of Teach's home to protect him and his students.

The Keeper never gave up what was his.

The Keeper's goons had drugged her and brought her back to a rundown, empty building that even a slumlord abandoned. It was even more run down than the last place he'd kept her.

He was punishing her.

A lone bed set on a cold concrete floor. One dresser and one small closet held the new clothes he'd bought her to wear for the higher paying clients. A vanity with a wash bowl leaned haphazardly against the wall in the bathroom. The commode wouldn't flush. The room was windowless. Trash littered the floor. No electricity. No heat or running water. Only rats and the horrible stench.

And, a bolted door.

Oh God. Why hadn't she given Teach more details on where The Keeper had taken her in the beginning? It would've at least given them a place to start looking. She had been so ashamed at the time and wanted to hide her six-month nightmare. But, look where it had gotten her. Back into the hellhole Gator had rescued her from.

The Keeper vowed revenge against Teach and punished her unmercifully for his loss in income over the last weeks. Even though she was bruised and battered the Keeper kept the men coming for twelve hours straight. One after another.

Until, she passed out.

"Mama, I'm sorry" were her last thoughts until she'd woken moments before with no man lying on top of her.

And, now Annie heard The Keeper's heavy footsteps as he neared where she was laying in pain.

"Little Annie, little Annie. Wakie, Wakie. You can't fool me. I know you're awake. I've brought you some food. You need to keep your strength up for later. I have more men waiting for your sweet, young charms. You've became very popular, you know. The men wants you." His voice hardened and his eyes turned glacier. He grabbed her tangled hair and jerked. "Sit up and eat. Then, we need to get you cleaned up. You smell and look like a whore. No man will want you stinking like this."

Her eyes flew open. He stood before her, his six foot large frame, black hair, graying at the temples, cold, blue eyes, wearing an expensive suit and leather shoes. He was her demon, her worst nightmare when once he was her Prince.

"Please God, help me."

The Keeper clutched his crotch. "This is the only god who will help you from now on. Get used to it."

Little Annie believed him. "Oh, Mama. I'm so sorry."

CHAPTER ELEVEN

Gator and Cruiser arrived back at Teach's around midnight, both boys hungry and exhausted. Teach was still awake and waiting for them. From the forlorn look on their faces, he knew the outcome of their search. His heart fell. Dammit.

Tears gathered in Gator's eyes and he furiously wiped them away. His sneakered feet shuffled. His Cajun accent was more intent from his weariness and softer heart. "We couldn't find her, Teach. It's like Annie disappeared from the face of the earth. None of our contacts have seen her and after me and Cruiser put out the word, they've been looking and asking around. Nothing."

Cruiser ran a tired hand through his purple Mohawk and added, "Teach, the word on the street is the guy Annie called The Keeper has it in for you for stealing his money maker. Annie. He's been asking questions, but no one in our tight-fisted alliance is telling him anything and it's pissing him off. They know nothing about this prick head. It's like he popped up out of nowhere."

Teach shook his head. "He can't hide forever. We'll find him. What else?"

Cruiser shrugged. "He has his own backers, man. His men's been bragging to anyone who'll listen. Says he vows to bring you down and take over all of your profitable enterprises. And, knock you from your throne."

Teach snorted. "And, become the King of the Alley thieves? Come on. This guy is crazy. He doesn't have a clue to what I do and never will. Sounds like he wants a pissing contest with me."

Gator chuckled and wiped his moist eyes. "He wouldn't stand a chance. You're the best at what you do."

Teach shook his head. "Correction. We're the best. I couldn't do it without my students."

Cruiser leaned against the office wall, his eyes drooped. "So Teach, what'cha gonna do about this psycho?"

"Teach him a lesson he'll never forget, after we get Annie back. Now, you boys get something to eat in the kitchen and then go on up and get some sleep. Quit worrying. I'll take care of everything," Teach told them.

A plan was already formulating.

* * *

Tuesday morning brought Tara and Dobbs no closer to solving the murder case. Tara propped her feet on her desk and stared at her crime board while she waited on Dobbs to arrive back from the forensic lab. They were checking for hopeful fingerprints found from the scenes of the recent robberies and the murder/robbery case they were working on, now. She wouldn't hold her breath they would find any similar prints or any print at all, but they needed to try.

Tara rummaged around in her desk drawer for enough change to buy a package of donuts out of the vending machine around the corner to go with her much needed coffee. She might half them with Dobbs. Or not. She was starving.

Before she could find what she needed her cell phone rang. Abandoning her search, she picked up her phone. "Detective Woods."

"I want to report a missing girl." The baritone voice on the other end of the line was muffled and undistinguishable.

"Sir, that would be the Missing Persons department. This is homicide. Let me transfer you."

"No. No...I need you Detective Woods and your partner, Detective Dobbs. No one else."

"Sorry. I can't help you. Not my jurisdiction, but the detectives in Missing Persons are more than qualified to assist you. Let me send you through to them." Tara transferred him and hung up. Really. She had enough on her plate without doing everyone else's job in the precinct.

Before she could stand with the change she'd found for the vending machine, her cell phone rang, again. "You help me find Annie and I'll give you the name of the robbers you're looking for." The same strong voice as before.

"How do you know about the robbers? Who are you?" Tara sat up on alert and motioned for quiet as Dobbs strolled into her office. "Put a trace on this call." She mouthed to her partner.

"Never mind who I am. The words out on the street. The person who has my Annie is the one behind the recent robberies and the murder of that older couple, Senator Chambers' parents over the weekend. They call him The Keeper. You find Annie and you'll find your murderer who robbed them before stabbing them to death."

"I don't know you from the next crazy prick in New York and I don't believe a word you're saying."

"I don't give a fucking shit whether you believe me or not. But, think about this, a wonderful young girl is going to die because you can't trust what I'm telling you. Then, guess what? It will be a homicide case. Is that what you're waiting for? Maybe you're right. Maybe you're not the brilliant detective I thought you were."

"You're out of line." Tara's anger rose. She stood and paced her office floor when Dobbs shook his head. No trace on the phone. A disposable. Pay per minute phone that was untraceable. The number wouldn't display on her phone. Just her damn luck.

"Okay. If I decide to help you, I'll need your name, address and phone number. And, this Annie's last name."

"Not happening. You'll have to trust me."

"You must think I'm a fool. Anyone who can read a newspaper knows we're investigating this murder. I'm in no mood to go on a wild goose chase every time a nut case comes out of the woodwork spewing a lot of made-up crap. Give me something more concrete if you want me to believe you."

Silence for a long moment. Then, "The wedding rings stolen were matching rose gold antique wedding rings and band. Her wedding ring had six diamonds, four square emeralds and two oval garnets. Mid-Victorian era. One of the oil paintings was a ocean landscape. The other was of children playing on the cobblestone streets of Madrid. The Keeper is in the process of fencing them. Is that enough proof for you, Detective?"

Without responding to his sarcasm, she snapped. "Where do you want to meet and talk this over?"

"Not happening. I'll be in touch over the phone. You'll need me to teach and guide you in finding Annie. Granted, you may have a little understanding of what is kept hidden in the back alleys of New York. But, you have no clue about the real life the desperate teen runaways and the homeless lead every day in the dark underworld. Cops know nothing about their secrets, man. You don't learn this kind of lifestyle in academy or walking the beat. You learn it by living it. Don't try to go it alone, Detective. We're a tight knit family. They won't let you into their well-kept secrets unless I give the okay. Trust me."

The phone went dead.

CHAPTER TWELVE

Tara ran her fingertips across her scalp in frustration and told Dobbs everything said over the phone. She paced the floor.

Dobbs bounced the eraser end of his pencil on the desk as he worked the new information through his mind. "At this point we have nothing else to go on. What do we have to lose?"

Tara shot a glance at her partner. "Our lives maybe? This guy sounds like a psycho."

Dobbs nodded in agreement. "But, a psycho who knows things about our case that we haven't released to the public. How else would he be able to give us an accurate description of the stolen goods unless he'd seen them?"

"Because he or this phantom named The Keeper is the one who stole or fenced them, maybe?" Tara was tempted to add 'Duh?', but decided Dobbs wouldn't hesitate to throw the immature remark back into her face.

Dobbs grinned like he knew exactly what she'd left out of her snide remark. They'd been partners too damn long, she decided.

She continued. "I say we do it both ways. Follow the leads we already have, check into the markets Jake suggested on the paintings, work closer with Detective Landers on the recent robberies and wait for a phone call from a psycho. Until we have a last name on this missing girl, Annie it won't do us any good to have Melinda run her name on the National missing teen and runaway database. Not much we can do until he calls back,··· if he calls back."

Dobbs stretched out his long legs in front of him. "I think he'll call. What I want to know is how he got a hold of your cell phone number. And, why you?"

Tara shrugged. "No mystery there. My phone number is on my business card just like yours. We hand them out like candy to our witnesses or anyone who might know something about a case we're working on. He knows we're working this murder slash robbery case. It only makes sense that he would contact me first."

"True. So, he had one of your cards. That would mean you've talked to him face to face. But when and where?"

"Good question. Anytime between now and five years, ago when I became Detective. Needle in a haystack." Tara stood and crossed the floor to her crime board. Dobbs was right. They couldn't let any leads, slim though it might be slip through their fingers.

She began moving the pictures of the murdered couple around, pairing them with the other guests at the party the elderly Chambers had gone to. Then, she connected them with the guests of the charity benefit the younger Senator Chambers and his wife attended. They all knew each other. According to the Senator they were all good friends who could easily afford the paintings themselves. Why steal?

Unless, killing the couple was their plan all along and they robbed only to cover up their true intent. The recent burst of robberies had been on every TV station and local newspapers around. They could've easily copycatted and used the knowledge they'd learned to throw the NYPD off their tracks. But, what would be their true motive? Things weren't adding up to her.

Frustrated, Tara sighed and turned back to Dobbs. "We may be wasting our time with these people on the crime board, but let's call in our officers assigned to us for a quick meeting. I want to know what they found out when they interviewed the guests a second time. Say 1:00?"

Dobbs stood and stretched. "Sounds like a plan. I'll start calling. Let's bring Detective Landers into the meeting, as well. You never know when some of the information we think is irrelevant may be an important piece of information to Landers."

Tara sighed and grabbed her car keys. "You're right. If he's readily available, we'll need his help. While you're doing that, I'll run and grab us a sandwich on the corner. I'm starving."

"Make mine a double meat."

"Should've known." Tara shook her head and headed out. It wasn't fair. They both spent the same amount of time in the gym each day. Dobbs wouldn't gain a pound after eating that much carbs and fat. She'll probably gain two pounds just watching him eat his big lunch.

Before she could step out of the office, Tara's phone rang and all thoughts of food in the near future disappeared. She walked back to her desk and picked up the phone. "Detective Woods."

"Tara, this is Ben. Sorry it's taken me so long to get back to you, but I've got something I think you two will be interested in."

"Great. Dobbs is here. Let me put you on speaker phone," she told the Medical Examiner. "Alright, go ahead."

"I've just completed the autopsy of both victims. Both died from multiple stab wounds and as we suspected they were consistent to the cuts from a six-inch stiletto switchblade. But, here's the kicker. I found skin beneath the male's fingernails. His nails are split and torn. I would say he fought his assailant and collected some DNA. I'm sending everything to the lab right now."

Tara and Dobb both did a fist pump and broke out into laughter. Finally, some evidence that might help solve the case. "Ben, if you were close by I would give you a big kiss on the lips, right now. We owe you one."

"You're not getting a kiss from me, but I'd gladly buy you a drink. Thanks man." Dobbs added.

Ben laughed. "I'll accept the kiss and the drink. Glad I could be of help. Good luck finding the bastards." He hung up.

Tara grinned and dialed the number to their forensic lab. When the technician answered, she asked for a rush job on the information Ben was sending them. The sooner the better. Keeping her fingers crossed that the DNA found would match up to the National Database records and their case would be solved.

But, Tara wasn't holding her breath. Cases were never that easy or simple. Her stomach grumbled reminding her where she'd been heading before Ben called. Grabbing her car keys, she tossed them into the air and caught them. "Lunch time."

Once again she headed out of her office to pick up their sandwiches for lunch. Double meat sounded pretty good right now.

* * *

Teach, Gator, Striker, BoneZ and Cruiser sat in Teach's white SUV down the street at a safe distance from the police station. They watched through dark tinted glass as Detective Tara Woods made her way to the corner food truck.

Laid back, portraying someone who didn't have a care in the world, Striker asked, "Do you think she bought your story, Teach?"

Bored from the long surveillance of the police station, Teach shifted in his seat until he was comfortable. He glanced at Striker in the passenger side. "I hope to hell not. If she's as smart as I'm hoping, she'll be more than cautious. So will her partner. But, in the end she'll realize I'm the Teacher and they are my students in finding Annie. That's my one and only goal. Finding Annie."

Striker shifted uncomfortably in his seat, but never uttered his own thoughts. True, he wanted to find Annie as much as the others. But, remaining out of the slammer was his ultimate goal.

CHAPTER THIRTEEN

Annie curled her tiny body into a tight ball and moaned. Her right eye was swollen shut and the inside of her thighs were bruised and sore.

Her last john got off on inflicting pain. It was the only way he could finish. He was one of The Keeper's best paying customers and unfortunately one she'd known in the past; before she'd run away from The Keeper.

Annie stifled a whimper and tried to listen for any sound outside the room. The john had left a short while earlier. But, The Keeper hadn't showed up as usual to taunt her or bind her hands and feet until it was time to clean her up for the next customer.

She'd lost all sense of time. She didn't know how many hours or days had passed since she'd been snatched from her hiding place. One day? Two? With the room's continual darkness, she wasn't sure.

It was senseless to ask for help. She'd learned her lesson the first time after begging the first john to rescue her. She still felt the sharp pain from the Keeper's fist slamming into her stomach. His cruel streak escalated to a higher level after she'd ran away and Teach took her in. Now, that he had her back into his clutches he made her pay for leaving him with harsh frequent punishments.

But, it wouldn't keep her from trying to escape if the opportunity presented itself. She had to believe Teach and the boys were looking for her, but she couldn't depend on them getting to her in time. She could only depend on herself. As always. The Keeper's temperament was too volatile. She had to get away, somehow.

And soon.

Annie lay still for a long moment in the darkness allowing her hearing, her only useable sensory to become more astute.

Where was the Keeper?

With care, she inched her legs off the side of the bed. Taking several steady breaths, she tried to stand. The excruciating pain forced her back down. Tears fell unchecked down her face, her bruised eye burning.

"I'm stronger than this. I can do it. I have to do it. Please God, help me." She whispered her prayer and tried to stand, again. She didn't know how much time she would have before he or his men returned.

This time she managed to stand on shaky legs. She held her bruised stomach with one hand and placed her other hand on the wobbly dresser beside the bed to steady herself. She blew out a painful breath and took a step toward the door.

The Keeper hadn't been back to lock the door after the last man had left and she hoped it was still unlocked. This was her only chance and she had to take it. Now.

Where was the Keeper?

Annie took another step. And, then another. Her strung nerves pushed her on. Her breath came out in hurried pants. She grabbed a hold of the bed's foot post and took another step.

Six more feet and she could escape. She wiped the blinding tears from her eyes and took another step.

And, then another.

Four more steps.

The door swung open.

"Going somewhere?"

Annie screamed and scrambled backwards. The back of her knees hit the bed and she fell backwards onto the mattress, her heart beating out of her chest. The bright light from the doorway blinded her.

Then, she heard a whimper and a body fell beside her.

The Keeper laughed, an evil sound. "I brought you some company. Becky here needs a roommate and you're it, Annie." He grabbed her ankles and tied them together and then her hands using the rope restraints hooked to the headboard. He grabbed the other girl's rope and did the same.

"Now, you two girls get to know each other while I have your meals sent in. Have fun." The Keeper laughed and turned to leave the room. Then, turned back to Annie, all laughter gone. "You'll pay for trying to leave me, Annie. The next time, I'll kill you."

Annie heard the door open and shut. The lock clicked into place.

* * *

At 1:00 sharp, Officer Jackson, Deputy Officer Banks and Detective Landers entered the small conference/break room and sat across the long table from Tara and Dobbs. Tara opened her notebook and glanced up at the officers. "Give us an update."

Jackson checked his notes. "Banks and I interviewed the remaining fifteen guests at Larry and Kay Brightons shindig. Seven married couples and one single man. They vouched for each other claiming they all stayed until around midnight or later that night. Two couples had babysitters who were able to tell us what time they arrived home and it was after midnight. The Chambers bid them goodnight a little after ten. According to the guests, the couple didn't seem upset or nervous like they were afraid of anyone. Nothing out of the ordinary. He just didn't feel well and they left early. None of the guests deviated from the story they gave you in the initial interview the next morning."

Banks added, "The one single guest, Chase Masters stated that he'd offered at one time to buy several paintings from Mr. Chambers, but he had refused to sell."

Tara leaned forward. "So, he had seen the paintings in their home?"

"Yes. The elder Chambers hosted a few parties and Masters had been invited along with the other guests who had been at the Brightons'. I think his statement was, quote," He should've sold them to me. His loss." unquote," Banks told her.

"A good friend, there." Dobbs shook his head, disgust written all over him. "What do we know about Masters?"

Jackson searched his notes. "He owns an upscale real estate business downtown. He'd had dealings with all of the guests either buying or selling them homes and a couple of large commercial sites. No one we interviewed really knew much about his past and he was very vague when we asked. He told us his parents died when he was young and his mother's sister took him in and raised him. He gave us the sister's name. We're checking that out. That's all we know right now."

Tara rubbed her chin and leaned back. "Did he mention any of the paintings specifically? Describe them in anyway?"

Jackson glanced at his notes, again. "Yes. He mentioned one was of an ocean view he wanted for the foyer in his home."

Tara slid a glance toward Dobbs and then back to Jackson. "We never told anyone which paintings were stolen. A little funny he mentioned the one we're looking for. Jackson, see what else you can find out about him. Something about him rubbed me wrong when I first interviewed him and I'm thinking even less of him now. Who knows? A cop's instinct, maybe."

Detective Landers spoke up. "Paintings and jewelry are common items stolen from the other residents I'm investigating. It sounds like this Masters knows his art. I'd like to know where he was during the other robberies I'm investigating. At least rule him out. I'll run a check on him through the robbery database, too. If he has a record with the law, I'll find him."

"Thanks. That will help. Anything else, guys?"

"That's all we know," Jackson told her.

"Great start. Keep looking and keep us updated on your finds. Good work." Tara thanked them as they rose to leave.

Everyone filed out of the room. Tara and Dobbs remained sitting at the table. Dobbs turned to her and said. "You know you're fishing with an empty hook. Just because Masters knew about the painting doesn't mean he's involved in the robbery or murder. He had a solid alibi. He never left the party until after the murder."

Tara sighed and stood and walked toward the door. "I know. But, I didn't like the man from the first moment I laid eyes on him. Something about the way he stared at me at the Senator's home gave me the creeps. We may not connect him to the murder, but I bet he's done something wrong we can charge him with."

Dobbs laughed and followed. "The poor man stared wrong at the wrong woman, so now he's a criminal."

"You've got that right."

CHAPTER FOURTEEN

Tara tapped her pen in a rapid motion against her desk, deep in thought. Suddenly, she stood. Without glancing at Dobbs, she made her way to the door. "That crime board isn't telling us anything. The phone hasn't rung, our case is getting cold and I'm going stir crazy. Let's hit the road."

Dobbs swung his legs off the desk and stood. "Right behind you, Partner."

Moments later, Tara climbed in behind the wheel of her assigned Camry with Dobbs beside her. After buckling up, she drove out of the nearly empty parking lot and headed north.

"Mind telling me where we're going?"

"Downtown Manhattan."

Dobbs glanced her way. "Got a reason?"

"Yep. We have several informants on the streets. Seems like a good time to use one." Tara knew Dobbs was studying her, many questions probably flying through his mind. She entered the heavy interstate traffic, sped up and moved into the center lane before Dobbs responded.

"So, you are. I knew it. He's got to you."

"I am what?"

"You're going to hunt for this girl before the mystery caller calls back and I didn't hear you deny that he got to you."

Tara shrugged a shoulder, glanced out her side mirror and changed lanes. "Wrong on both counts. Not I, but *we* are going to hunt for Annie and he didn't get to me. The girl, Annie did. If there's a slight chance she's real and in danger, I want to do what I can to save her. We need to follow up on all leads. If finding her helps us find the murderer, it's a win, win. We've put the other two unsolved cases from ten years, ago on the back burner until this is solved, so we need to get cracking on this one." She couldn't deny it. This story tugged at her heart strings. She knew how it felt to be so helpless.

"Say, I agree...."

Tara's hand flew to her heart. "Oh, my God. A first. He's agreeing with me."

Dobbs grinned. "Don't expect it to happen, again. As I was saying, we can't trust this guy. I know I was all for working with the creep at first, but I'm having second thoughts. We don't know anything about him. He called you out of the blue with this wild story about a missing girl he wants us to locate. Why didn't he report it to missing persons like a normal person? I don't know, Tara. It could be a setup."

"I know. That's why I want to meet with our informant. If anything is out on the street about the paintings or this Annie, Shorty will have heard it."

"Maybe. If we can locate him." Dobbs phone rang. He answered, "Dobbs."

Tara glanced his way and notice a smile forming on his face and heard a female voice over the phone. She turned down the radio.

"Jenna, I'm glad you called." His voice softened to almost a whisper.

"I was hoping you would've called my by now. I really enjoyed the other night," Jenna purred through the phone line.

"I enjoyed it, too. I'm sorry I haven't gotten back with you. This latest murder case have kept us busy We've been working⋯."

She cut him off mid-sentence. "Listen, the reason I called, a few friends and I are meeting tonight at Charros. I was hoping you could join us. The two of us could go back to my apartment later and have a little alone time."

Tara watched him squirm in his seat. He glanced her way. She didn't bother hiding her grin. She knew he would have to beg his way out of this date, too. Jenna was the latest woman in Dobbs' revolving door love life. In and out. Tara didn't have much hope for this one staying long.

Dobbs sighed and glanced out his window. "I would love to, but I'll be working late. Can I call you and make another date for later?"

Silence. Then, her voice rose. "No, Matt. Don't bother. This is the second time you've bowed out on me. I don't do part time love affairs. It's all or nothing for me. There's always someone else who can take your place. I hope you know what you're missing. Goodbye Matt." The phone call ended.

Tara kept her silence and allowed Dobbs a little brooding time. Relationships sucked in their line of work. She was often amazed that Jake was so understanding. They made time for themselves when they could and each minute was more precious than the last.

But, Dobbs hadn't met that one special someone who was willing to wait on the sidelines until the murder case was solved. Or, know that another case will soon follow and not get out of sorts over it.

Normally, that didn't bother him. Dobbs was a love 'em and leave 'em type of lover. He bounced back easily from one relationship to another. With his golden, bad boy good looks, he never had a problem finding someone to share his bed and he took advantage of it. Tara fretted he would never settle down with one woman.

She and Dobbs were perfect partners with careers meaning everything to both of them.

Detective work was their life. They teased each other unmercifully and sometimes a sexual current went through them, the partner syndrome, but they always cut it off well before it got out of hand. They always had each other's back.

She only hoped he would meet that one special person to go home to at night. He volunteered as a Little League baseball coach every year and participated in several youth organizations. He would make a great dad, someday.

Tara exited the interstate and drove at a creeping pace down a side street in a slum neighborhood. The area was run down with homeless cardboard shelters lining the graffiti covered walls. Trash littered the streets. Rats and cockroaches scurried everywhere.

She pulled over, parked and unhooked her seat belt. "So, let's find Shorty. We'll check his usual hangout first."

Dobbs finally glanced her way and nodded. He grumbled. "Sure. As you probably enjoyed eavesdropping from my conversation with Jenna, I don't have anything more exciting to do. Walking down a life-threatening hood to find a thieving snitch is a helluva lot more satisfying than my sex life, right now. I do love my job."

Tara grinned. "Quit whining and the next time take your phone off speaker if you don't want me to listen in to your pitiful conversations."

She stepped out watching for rats. Her grin faded and she shuddered. She hated rats. Why couldn't Shorty hang out a couple blocks over in the nicer area?

They crossed the street and entered a dive bar that hadn't been taken over by the classier establishments. The dimly lit, grungy room smelled of cigarette smoke and body odor. One was against the law and the other should be, she thought.

The seedy bar catered to motorcycle gangs, lowlifes and criminals. It must've been a slow evening. A couple of thugs in leather and chaps sat at the bar. Four heavily tattooed thugs sat at a back booth with the table covered in empty beer bottles. Two more played a game of pool. Loud, drunken laughter and conversation filled the room and then went dead silent as the patrons smelled a cop entering the room.

Tara's hand lingered on the cold steel of her gun. Dobbs stood close to her side glancing around. The only sound in the room came from the bartender hastily moving to the other end of the bar.

Dobbs nudged her and pointed to the back of the dark room where a man stood. "There's Shorty. Aaaahhhh, damn it, he's running and I'm wearing my boots."

Tara and Dobbs took off running after Shorty, all six foot and eight inches of him.

CHAPTER FIFTEEN

Dobbs chased Shorty several blocks down the broken sidewalk while Tara rushed to the car. She caught up with them a few minutes later.

Dobbs had Shorty on the ground and handcuffed. Both were breathing heavily from their exertion. Dobbs rose and helped their informant to his feet and then into the backseat of the car. He slid in beside him.

Tara drove off.

"Damn it, Dobbs. Did you have to tackle me to the ground, man? Ain't I always helped you. I don't need this kind of treatment. Shiiiiiiiiitttt."

Dobbs shrugged and glanced at Shorty. His pale, pocked face was red and his huge, bulb nose was off-centered from being broken at least once or more. His clothes too small for his massive body smelled of body odor and his breath was bad enough to ward off the devil.

Dobbs leaned back breathing hard. "I got tired of chasing you."

Shorty huffed up and turned his back to him. "Get these handcuffs off of me. No one will see us here. How many times do I have to tell you to get bigger handcuffs? Are you trying to break my wrists?"

Dobbs dug his keys out of his pocket and unlocked the handcuffs. "Have you ever thought about losing some weight? Tackling a three hundred pound giant isn't something I enjoy. That's why I quit football in high school," Dobbs grumbled.

Tara drove on to the interstate and glanced into her rearview mirror at the two men sitting in the back seat. "Will you two quit arguing? Shorty, what's the word out on the street about a recent art and jewelry heist or about a runaway girl named Annie who's missing?"

Shorty settled back into his seat and rubbed his wrists while he thought. "Very little. A few whispers about the sloppy work done on the hit, but nothing more. That couple shouldn't have been killed. A botched robbery is what I heard. Then recently, a couple of young guys searched on the streets for a girl they called Annie. No one has seen her in several weeks. Words out that several teens are missing off the streets, but that's not unusual. What's unusual is the recent increase in missing teens."

Dobbs raised a brow and glanced toward Tara and then back to Shorty. "Sex trafficking, a multi-million business around here."

Shorty nodded. "Yeah, that's what I heard. The teens, both girls and boys are used in a local prostitution ring for a while and then sold to bring in fresher faces."

"Any names being thrown around?" Tara asked.

"Babe...."

Tara's sharp glance met his in the rearview. "It's Detective to you. Now, answer my question."

Shorty raised his beefy hands in mock surrender. "Okay. Okay. Sorry, Detective Babe. You know I don't give names."

Tara snarled.

Dobbs grinned. "Shorty, don't you know not to mess with a woman with a gun?" He pulled out his billfold and pulled out two twenties. "Will this help?"

Shorty snapped the money from Dobbs' fingertips and stuffed it into his torn shirt pocket. He tapped his pocket. "That's just enough for one name. He goes by the name The Keeper. I've heard he's one mean son of a bitch. But, you won't ever find him. The boys looking for this Annie said she was missing and figured The Keeper had her. Their boss wanted her back. The

Keeper is out for revenge against the man who took her in when she'd fled him. "

"What's this Keeper's real name?"

"They didn't say."

"Who were these boys?"

Shorty shrugged with a nervous glance behind him. "I said it was worth one name. I gave you the name."

Dobbs reached back into his billfold.

Shorty raised his hand to stop him. Turning serious, he said, "You know as well as I do no one gives their real names on the streets. Tara, Dobbs...these are some bad ass dudes looking for Annie. And, one bad ass who might have her. Don't underestimate these dude's survival skills or the real threat to anyone getting too close."

" Who's the boy's boss? At least give us that." Dobbs said ignoring the warning.

Shorty glanced out the side window. His lips thinned before turning back to Dobbs. "They call him Teach. He brings runaways into his home and teaches them survival skills and the art of theft and fencing. Hence, the name Teach. But, man..., he's like Batman. No one other than his students knows where he disappears to or really what he looks like. He stays in the dark and wears a hoodie covering his face. He's scary, man and his students are loyal. You won't ever get past them to get to him. That's all I'm saying, man."

"Wanna make a bet?" Tara exited the off ramp and circled around. She drove back a couple of blocks further from where she'd picked up Shorty and Dobbs and let the informant out. They had gotten all of the information from him that he was willing to give. The two names he'd given them was a good start.

* * *

Young Ellen climbed out of the rusty dumpster sitting in the alley behind a family restaurant that closed minutes before. It smelled of rotten cabbage and other spoiled foods of the day, but she was too hungry to care. She gripped a slice of cake in one dirty hand and slid back into the darkness. Today she would celebrate her fourteenth birthday and the ten day anniversary of becoming a runaway.

Climbing into her makeshift shelter of cardboard and plastic, Ellen sat cross-legged on the cold, hard ground and enjoyed the chocolate cake. She licked the cream icing off her chapped lips and dirty fingers and ignored the tears streaming down her face. She didn't need her mother's damn chocolate cake for her birthday or the money daddy slipped into a birthday card every year.

She was free.

She was no longer stifled by her parent's strict rules. She could come and go as she damn well pleased. Date a boy. Have a life. Smoke.

Drink. Whatever. No more rules. No one to ground her to her bedroom, now.

No more hick town Nebraska.

She was free.

Ellen furiously wiped the tears from her eyes and crawled out of her temporary home for the night. She wouldn't have to live here long. She would be somebody someday. She'd show them. She might even forgive her parents one day and invite them to visit her in her mansion when she makes it big as a New York best-selling author.

Just wait and see.

Her spirits rose a little but, now she was thirsty. A water faucet was behind the restaurant's outside wall and she walked toward it. Reaching the faucet, she turned the knob and scooped the water into her hands and drank. Satisfied, she wiped the water from her mouth and turned off the faucet. She was tired and with her tummy full it was time for bed.

She stood and turned.

And, then she saw him, a mere second before she was doomed.

Large hands grabbed her. One hand covered her mouth. Her unknown assailant dragged her flailing body further into the darkness, far enough that no one she knew and loved would ever see her again.

CHAPTER SIXTEEN

Back in the office bright and early Wednesday morning Tara yawned and grabbed the coffee pot. She filled two cups of freshly brewed coffee and handed one cup to Dobbs. "I didn't sleep much last night. The conversation with Shorty yesterday kept rolling over and over in my mind. I think I was too exhausted to think straight." She rubbed her forehead feeling a headache coming on.

She reached into her desk drawer and popped two ibuprofens into her mouth and swallowed them dry. "There's something he said that keeps bothering me and I can't put my finger on it."

Dobbs blew on his coffee and glanced over the steaming cup at Tara. He propped his booted feet on her desk. "Maybe it's the missing girls who's bothering you. This is our second case in several months where teen girls have come up missing. We solved the other one. We'll solve this one."

"I don't think that's it." Thoughtfully, Tara shrugged and stared out of her office window.

The parking lot was beginning to fill with the dayshift officers coming on duty. The morning was already warm and humid. A perfect day for a storm to hit.

She pulled her hair back into a ponytail and sat down behind her desk. She took a sip of the warm brew. And, then another. She felt the cobwebs in her mind and her headache start to dissipate.

"The conversation keeps replaying in my mind. Something he said···.holy crap. That's it." She sat straight up. A spark of excitement flickered in her eyes as she glanced at Dobbs. "Shorty said the guy's name was Teach."

Dobbs right brow rose. "Yeah? So?"

"Don't you get it. The phone call from my mystery man said he was going to teach me how to find these girls. Teach me. Dobbs, it's the same guy. I know it."

"You're grabbing at straws."

"No. I'm not. Think about it, Dobbs. Mystery man and this Teach are both looking for Annie. It's too much of a coincidence. They're one and the same. I know it. I don't know why this didn't hit me sooner. It was right in front of my eyes and I missed it. Damn it, I missed it."

"Don't beat yourself up over it. We were pretty occupied until late last night trying to locate Keeper. Now, say I agree with you, it's still not much help. We could roam the New York streets forever looking for this Teach, but if it's like Shorty said, no one knows what he looks like or where he lives."

Tara grinned and sat back in her seat. "We don't have to look for him. He's found us and has my cell phone number. Right now, he needs us to help find Annie. He'll call. And, hopefully lead us to this slime bag Keeper who happens to be our main suspect on the murder case, according to Teach."

Dobbs snorted. "You're going to believe this Teach? You do realize Shorty said this guy was a thief, don't you?"

"Yes, smart butt, I heard what he said, but he said Teach was a thief, not a murderer. If he lives off the street, I would think he deals in small time thefts. Maybe a pick pocket or car theft, but not fine art. And, how would he know the Chamber's routine?"

Dobb's shoulder lifted as he walk toward his office. "I'm not saying he did it. I'm saying we don't need to cross him off the list."

* * *

Teach sat at his long, elegant dining-room table eating a large breakfast. Quiet and subdued, his students sat around the table, their thoughts on little Annie.

Finished eating, Teach pushed his plate back and drained his coffee cup. Using his cloth napkin to wipe his mouth, he glanced around the table and cleared his throat. "I've made a decision."

Striker glanced up from his plate. "What's that, Teach?"

"We're going to ditch the hit for Saturday night."

All four boys started arguing at once.

Once again, Striker as the second-in-command summed up all of their arguments in three sentences. "Don't you think we should have a say so in that decision? That's a week without a paycheck for us. You're hurting our pockets, man."

The Teach's eyes narrowed and his fist clenched.

Striker flinched.

Then, Teach calmly placed the palms of his hands on the table top and glanced at his students, one young face at a time. He spoke softly, as soft as a switchblade slicing through meaty flesh. "Students, if you hadn't failed my class on the last robbery I wouldn't be skipping this one. You boys got a fucking 'F'. Don't expect me to reward you for your dismal failure. You're lucky I didn't kill you instead of allowing you to live under my roof rent free and eat up my food. Now, because of your stupid incompetence, I have two detectives sniffing around my ass. And, until I can come up with a sure fire plan to get us out of this mess, we're lying low. Got me?"

"Yes Sir." The four boys answered and shifted in their seats knowing better than to question his authority.

"Good. Now, let's use our energy on trying to locate Annie. I've planted a small seed in Detective Wood's mind that The Keeper is not only behind New York's human trafficking but, also the past robberies and the murder last Saturday night. We have to make the story believable."

"How do we do that, Teach?" BoneZ asked.

The Teach grinned and patted BoneZ on the back. "By using the resources we have, Son. Now, if you boys will excuse me, I have a phone call to make."

CHAPTER SEVENTEEN

Day? Night? Annie couldn't tell anymore. Nor, did she know what day it was. She'd lost all sense of time. It seemed like forever, but couldn't be more than a few days since she'd been brought here.

She scooted against the headboard and pulled her knees up to her chest holding them tight with her thin, trembling arms. She'd lost weight since she'd been there. But, at least he allowed her to bathe and wash her hair each day with a couple of pitchers of luke warm water he brought inside the room. She even had new clothes to wear when he took her to the hotels to meet with the special clients. The blouses were low cut and the skirts short, but they were clean.

Annie didn't know the name of the hotels or the clients. She only knew her clients asked specifically for her and the rooms were clean, smelled nice and had crisp clean sheets. No dump for sure.

She was blindfolded each time and driven to the location. The car she rode in smelled like new leather with roomy, cushy, heated seats beneath her. The Keeper enjoyed finer things, she noted.

Someone would lead her through a back entrance or somewhere no one would see her and take her into the darkened hotel room before the blindfold was removed. It was replaced after she serviced the client and was ready to leave.

Then, she was brought back here to service the disreputable, cheaper johns.

Annie looked out into the darkness of the room searching once again for a way to escape. She couldn't give up. She'd escaped once. She could do it, again. Even with the chance the Keeper would kill her if he caught her.

The other girl, Becky had been taken away after only a few hours in her room this morning. Annie was once again alone. The girl, incoherent from coming off a high had been no help.

Annie thought at first the two could work together, maybe overpower the Keeper and escape. But, the girl could do no more than shiver and moan, holding her stomach as the withdrawal pains consumed her.

Annie had taken care of her, bathing her drenched body and held her tight, whispering to her until the shivers calmed. Finally, when the girl settled into a deep sleep, the Keeper's goon came and took her away.

She knew in her heart she would never see Becky, again. She rested her cheek against her knees and wept. Wept for the girl. Wept for herself. She couldn't bear the thought of the pain she was putting her family through from her stupid, stupid, childish behavior. They wouldn't recognize their little girl, now. This baby had grown up hard and fast. Regret ran deep.

Annie swiped away the tears running down her cheeks. And, her family would know, she thought. They would know what she'd become. What she'd done.

They would know everything when they viewed her body at the morgue. If her body could be found.

* * *

Mid-day Wednesday in her office, Tara's cell phone rang just as she took a bite of her pastrami on rye. Swallowing, she glanced at Dobbs and answered.

"Detective Woods."

"I'm disappointed in you, Detectives. Is a washed out ex-football player your best source of information? More girls are missing, Detectives."

Tara put her phone on speaker. "Thank you...., Teach. Detective Dobbs is grateful to know he can out run and tackle a football player.

We were wondering about his past. Now, we know."

A long pause came over the phone.

"How did you know my name?"

"I'm glad you didn't deny it. I know a lot, Teach. But, I'm always open to learning new things. Why don't you tell us what you know about these missing girls and a guy they call The Keeper?"

"I take it you haven't found Annie. Why don't you tell us about your career as a thief after you tell us your real name?" Dobbs added.

Silence. Then, Teach responded with a short laugh. "I don't know what you're talking about. I'm no thief. You need a new informant if he told you I was. And, no. We haven't found Annie. But, let me tell you what I know. She's out there, hopefully alive and if we work together we can find her. Are you willing to agree that I know more about the runaways and white slavery trade than you do?"

"I agree you failed to tell us your name. I also agree you've had more experience living on the streets, but don't ever underestimate us, Teach. With that said, we're willing to work with you to an extent. But, if we ever find out your hands are dirty, we'll come looking for you and won't stop until we do. Are we clear?" Tara asked, her voice firm. She would never allow him to think he was in complete control.

Laughter erupted over the phone. "Detectives, if I thought you were stupid enough to *not* try to catch me, I wouldn't be asking you to work with me. But, you have to know, I don't plan on you ever finding me. If..., my hands were dirty. Now, that we're all on the same page, let me ask you both this, Detectives. Quiz number one for five points. Hundreds of runaway girls and boys in this city come up missing and taken out of the country each year. They're never seen, again. So, why do you think I believe Annie is still alive and in New York?"

Tara pulled at her bottom lip and glanced at Dobbs. She thought about the question. The obvious answer would be she'd contacted Teach, but Tara didn't think so. He would've mentioned that important piece of information right away.

"You told me over the phone yesterday that she ran away from The Keeper before your boys found her and you took her in. The Keeper went out of his way to find her and take her back. I would say she was special enough to him to keep her instead of selling her off. Am I right?"

"Maybe, they just had a lover's spat and she went back to The Keeper freely, " Dobbs added.

An expletive exploded over the phone. "No! Think about it, Dobbs. Annie was scared to death of him. She said he was evil. Tara's answer is correct. She gets the five points. Annie is special to him. But, why? Think about it."

"Glad we're on first name basis, now," Dobbs mumbled. He leaned back in his chair and rubbed his chin as he worked through his thoughts. "We know The Keeper is into prostitution and white slavery. Young girls and boys who have run away and living off the streets are his moneymakers."

"I agree. Money is all he cares about. So, Annie would make him more money as a prostitute than what he could make selling her, " Tara reasoned.

Dobbs nodded. "That would mean she's not bringing in nickels and dimes."

Tara continued his thoughts, a flicker of excitement grew. "Her clients are rich and asking solely for Annie. Maybe they've threatened to take their business elsewhere. The Keeper would lose a large amount of money and their respectable influence if he lost these clients. That's why he kidnapped her back and hid her out."

"Very good, students. You both made an A plus. Now, second question. Fill in the blank. These men are rich and ————————?"

"Powerful."

"Powerful."

"Correct. Both of you."

"Give me names, Teach," Tara demanded, tired of his game. She pushed back from her desk and stood, pacing the floor.

"I don't know."

"Bullshit." Dobbs glared at the phone, drumming his fingers on the desktop.

"If I knew I'd have already found her and brought her home. These clients of hers are powerful enough that people on the streets are too scared to say a word about them. Not even a whisper."

"Look, I agree you have a good point. There's a valid reason why he might not have sold her when he first had her in his clutches, but there's too many unanswered questions and it makes me nervous. We could be way off the mark," Tara warned.

"She may have just gone home. She could be on a bus now," Dobbs reasoned, but didn't sound convincing.

"No. She didn't have the money for one thing. And, without giving anything away to the media in her home town, I called asking if they'd seen her. They're keeping a close eye on the case, but she hasn't shown up. It would be big news for them in her small town in Kentucky. No, she's still in New York. I'm certain of it."

"So, back to your theory. How would the Keeper know these clients? I would imagine they would only seek the beautiful and young high class girls. Clean. Disease free." Tara shuddered remembering some of the girls she'd arrested off the streets in the past. Most were filthy, shot up with heroin and carrying sexual transmitted diseases they passed from one john to the next. Most went right back to the streets after being released from jail. A sad, dangerous way to live.

"From what Annie mentioned before, the Keeper wasn't picky about his johns as long as they had money to pay. He didn't care whether they were lowlifes or filthy rich. But, he kept his girls protected and clean to keep the money rolling in. And, I would think he would have to be able to move freely between the street life and the upscale ritzy part of town. Fit in with both worlds. With as much money as he's probably making, I don't see him living in a dump. No, he's living upscale, somewhere. Who knows? These clients could be either his partners or social friends. They trust him enough to keep their secrets and they keep his."

"And, they're high up enough that their sordid secrets being discovered would be a disaster. Do you know how many people in New York would fit those descriptions?" Dobbs asked.

Tara sighed and rubbed her tired eyes. "Thousands."

Dobbs nodded. "Exactly."

"Then, I'll let you two get started." The phone went dead.

CHAPTER EIGHTEEN

Tara clicked her mouse until she'd scrolled to the bottom of the Missing Persons registry page for the state of Kentucky. Only one Annie from Bowling Green was listed. She jotted down the information listed on the site about the girl. Annie Kay Reynolds, white female, age 16, ran away from home seven months, ago and had not been seen since. Could this be their girl?

A grainy picture of a girl with a slim, gaunt face, blonde hair and haunting blue eyes was posted beside her information. This Annie looked to be ten years old instead of the reported sixteen.

Tara uploaded the photo and information to her cell phone. She sent the photo to the phone number still showing she'd last received from Teach. She messaged, "Is this our Annie?"

Within seconds, he messaged back. "Yes. She's not as innocent looking now, but that's her. Good job, Student. I'll make copies of this and have some boys hand them out on the streets. "

Great. Now, Tara had a face to the girl's name even though she bristled at the 'Student' part. "I'll send it out, as well," she typed.

She emailed the information she'd gathered to all of the New York and surrounding borough precincts asking them to be on the lookout for Annie. She then alerted the Kentucky Missing Persons Bureau to let them know the missing girl had been last seen in New York.

During the call, Tara learned from the Bureau that when they touched base with Annie's parents Thursday they mentioned they were leaving Bowling Green Friday morning. They were heading to New York to look for their daughter on their own as they did every weekend since she'd left home.

Tara glanced up from her computer as Dobbs entered her office. "Look at this." She turned her computer around until he could see her screen.

Dobbs' brow rose. "Our Annie?"

"Yes. Teach confirmed. It's her." Tara filled him in while printing off the information she'd found. She stood and pinned the printed sheet to her crime board along with the murdered couple and suspects. "If Teach can be believed, which is in question, Annie's kidnapper could be involved in these murders along with the local robberies, human trafficking and prostitution."

Dobbs moved to stand beside her, glancing at the board. He rubbed his chin as he studied what they had on the case. "So, in theory we're still back at step one. The question we still have is; if this Keeper is our man, how did he know the Chambers would be gone Saturday night? This wasn't a five minute job, so he had to know or think he knew they would have plenty of time to commit the robbery and leave before the couple returned. I don't think murder would damage his conscious, but he wouldn't want the added inconvenience of dodging the law. He has too many hats in the fire to deal with unplanned trouble."

Tara glanced up at him. "So, you think now it was someone at the party who would see the couple when they arrived and left?"

"Yeah, I do. The Senator said his dad wasn't feeling well that night, so they left early. That would've thrown a kink in their plans."

"So, why didn't this person let his people know the couple had left the party? The robbers had at least twenty minutes to rush out before the Chambers arrived home. We know there were at least two men doing the robbing who each murdered their victim, plus possibly a lookout driver and the one at the party watching the Chambers. A quick phone call to the two inside or to the lookout would've prevented the murders. They would've had a clean get away."

Dobbs shrugged. "Party guy was too drunk, maybe? Or, couldn't get away from guests in time to call? Who knows?"

"I don't buy the first. If we go back to our original thoughts and The Keeper was at the party and if he is behind the murders, I don't think he would allow himself to lose control by drinking too much. He would want his finger on every pulse driving his business. His multi-million dollar illicit business would need a strong leader, one in command at all times. The second reason...., maybe. And, we're assuming he wanted to prevent the murders. What if the murders were his ulterior motive instead of the robberies? We may be way off course here. Maybe the murders didn't happen because of where the Chambers were, but who they knew."

Dobbs glanced sharply her way. "You're thinking they might have been killed because their son is the Senator?"

Tara shrugged. "Just thinking out loud. I'm trying to go over every scenario in my mind. But, it's a possibility, isn't it? Maybe the Senator didn't back someone wanting an important bill to pass or something similar. They may have threatened him and followed through."

"Yes, it's possible and another angle to work on. The only problem I see is that no threats have been made to the Senator or his family that we know about, even though I imagine he's pissed off several people in his career. If they killed the parents to make a statement they wouldn't try to cover it up as being a robbery. They would want the Senator to know specifically what happened and why."

Tara walked back to her desk and sat down, her thoughts jumbled. "That's true. And, I doubt the Senator would keep that he's being threatened or blackmailed from us. Not when he's wanting his parent's murderers brought to justice."

Dobbs shrugged and sat across from her. He leaned forward with his arms resting on her desk. "Or, so he says. It's time to pay him another visit to see if we can gather any more information from him. We can throw those questions and more at him to watch his reaction." Dobbs glanced at his watch. "3:00 o'clock. Hopefully we can catch him in his office before he leaves for the day or in between meetings."

"Sounds good to me." Tara booted down her computer and rose. "I'm ready."

* * *

Thirty minutes later, Tara and Dobbs entered the Senators reception area and were immediately escorted to the Senator's office by his young, chirpy receptionist. Senator Chambers stood as they entered. Hope rose in his eyes. He motioned to a couple of chairs facing his desk. "Please, have a seat. Have you found my parent's murderers, yet?"

Tara and Dobbs sat. Tara answered, "No, I'm afraid not. But, we haven't given up. We need to ask you a few more questions if you don't mind."

The Senator's pale face showed dark shadows beneath his eyes. His suit and tie were wrinkled as if today he didn't care about his appearance. A wadded up moist tissue lay beside his hand. The hope faded from his eyes. "Anything, if it will help you find those killers. They released both of my parent's bodies yesterday and both funerals will be day after tomorrow. I was hoping I could bury them with full closure knowing those bastards were behind bars. Or dead. I don't really care which." Moisture developed beneath his eyelids, but he quickly blinked them away. "What do you need to know?"

Tara knew how he felt. She'd lost both of her parents in a similar murder when she was only a child. You never got over such a tragedy.

She reached across his desk and plucked another tissue from the box and handed it to him without a word about the tears. "We're trying all angles and eliminating them as we go, Sir. Do you think it's possible your parents might have been killed for revenge or blackmail? Do you know of any enemies who might have done this to pay you back for anything? Or, even your father, a former Senator? An eye for an eye, sort of thing?"

"Of course I have enemies. So, did Dad. I don't know of a Senator who doesn't with the type of decisions we have to make daily. With every bill we pass or vote down, we're either making someone very happy or pissing someone off. But, do I think some nutcase has out a vengeance against me or my dad? No, I don't."

Dobbs watched the Senator's eyes as he talked. "Are you positive? You can't think of anyone? Anyone at the party your parents attended, maybe?"

The Senator's eyes jerked away, not meeting Dobbs' stare. "Of course not."

Dobbs turned toward Tara and she gave a slight nod.

The Senator lied.

CHAPTER NINETEEN

Without calling or giving a warning, two hours later Tara and Dobbs walked into Chase Masters' Real Estate Office on the top floor of a brownstone ten-story building.

White marble tile flooring, brass statues and large wall hangings represented the reception area. Several agent's offices with their name tags on the door branched off the main area.

A young woman with long, shiny hair, perfect if overdone makeup, wearing a low revealing top sat behind the horseshoe counter. She aimed a smile of appreciation towards Dobbs with only a cursory glance at Tara.

Tara swore the girl leaned forward to show Dobbs more of her assets before asking in a sultry voice, "May I help you?"

Tara spoke to bring the girls focus back to her. "Yes. We need to see Chase Masters. Is he in?"

"Yes, but...." The girl looked down at her appointment book. "I don't see anything scheduled for now. Do you have an appointment?"

Tara pulled out her badge and showed the receptionist. "This is our appointment. Detective Woods and Detective Dobbs. We're here on police business. Now, do you mind showing us to his office?"

The girl huffed and glanced at Dobbs for support.

He grinned and shrugged, keeping his silence.

"Now would be good," Tara said.

With a glare at Tara, the girl picked up the phone and punched a few numbers. "Sir, there's two detectives here to see you." She listened, then nodded. "Yes sir, I'll send them right in."

The girl stood, adjusted her short skirt and led them to a large office on the floor. The large, heavy mahogany door with a brass nameplate showing the name Chase Masters opened and he stood in the doorway.

"Detectives, come on in." A friendly, cultured voice greeted them.

Tara took in his tall stature, lean muscled body, blonde hair and eyes that reminded her of the color of a cop car's blue lights. He was young. Probably mid to late twenties, she figured.

He stepped back and waved them inside his office.

Tara looked around. Evidently, the real estate business was beginning to boom, again. She made note to herself to check into how he'd acquired his immense wealth at such an early age and in this recent economy.

His sleek, black suit matched his high-end executive office. Well made. The large, mahogany wood desk and matching bookcase took up half the office. An office mini putt golf green was laid out in front of the massive window overlooking the city. Even his room freshener smelled expensive. The scent was nothing like what she found at her local superstore.

No knick knacks, mementos or photos anywhere. Nothing to personalize the room to give her further familiarization of his character.

Both person and office were impressive, but overdone. Like someone moving to a big city with permanent dirt from across the tracks on the bottom of his feet, Tara thought. A person's true roots were hard to hide no matter how you dressed it up.

Masters invited them to sit in the two, black leather chairs facing his desk. He sat across from them with his hands clasped on top. With a frown, he glanced down at the gold Rolex on his wrist. "I only have a few minutes before my next client arrives. What can I help you with, Detectives?"

Cold and ruthless.

She'd seen the same hardened faces on worthless thugs and unethical businessmen she'd put behind bars, Tara thought. She believed in first impressions and was pleased hers hadn't changed any from the time she'd met him at the Senator's home, Sunday morning. Opposite of the icy chill in his gaze, the thousand dollar smile he was beaming at them right now was as fake as a bad politician. You couldn't trust them, but she'd learned to detect them.

Or, he could be as innocent as an emotionless new born baby. Giving the man the benefit of doubt, she nodded towards Dobbs signaling she wanted him to take the lead this time.

Dobbs turned on his keyboard tablet and placed it on his lap. He took his time to get his notes pulled up. He waited until Master's started to fidget before he began. "We understand you were a guest at Larry and Kay Brightons' party Saturday night."

Masters leaned back. He adjusted the cuff of his shirt and nodded politely. "Yes, I was. As I told your police officers, I was there until midnight or a little later. The Brightons couple as well as several other guests can back me up. I drove straight home afterwards." His clipped words were as stiff as his collar.

Dobbs made a note on his tablet before leaning back looking as if he had all the time in the world and this was only a social visit. A nice chit chat between men. "So, Chase...may I call you Chase?"

A curt nod. "Of course."

"Great. So, Chase, how well did you know the Chambers?"

Chase shrugged and pulled at his collar. "Pretty well, I guess. I've known them for a couple of years. We met at a mutual friend's social. We have many common friends and most of them were at the party Saturday night."

Dobbs checked his notes. "I'm sure after a while you would all become a close knit group. I believe you also told the officers about the paintings that were stolen." Dobbs leaned forward and stared him down. "How did you know which paintings were stolen? We never leaked that information to the media."

A smug smile emerged on Chase's face. "Nothing sinister. I know my art, Detectives and I knew what the paintings were worth. And, I've been a guest a few times in their home and they showed them to me. I tried to buy those paintings from them before, but they didn't want to sell. I know if I were a thief, those two paintings would've been the first things I would've grabbed because of their value." He spread his hands wide and grinned. "But, of course, I'm no thief."

"We'll see." Tara jumped in. She glanced around the office. "Looks like you're doing pretty well for yourself."

He straightened, a slight tick in one eye began. "The last I heard, earning a good living isn't a crime, Detective."

There it was, again. A quick flash of dislike appeared in his eyes before he masked the emotion, Tara noticed. She was beginning to wonder if he hated all women, or just her. Or maybe he thought she was beneath him and didn't deserve his respect. Either way, she was ready to push some buttons and forgot she'd asked Dobbs to take the lead.

"So, as a high end realtor, I would think you would have access to multi-million dollar homes."

Chase leaned back in his chair. The smirk was back. "I do. So, do the other five agents in my firm. So do a few other real estate firms. Your point, Detective? I'm a very busy man. I don't have time to play twenty questions."

Tara bristled, but kept her emotions in check. "Maybe you would rather spend your time down at the station answering the questions, Masters." Tara deliberately used his last name to show she wasn't there to be his friend.

Chase glanced at Dobbs and then back to Tara, a sliver of ice in his voice. "That won't be necessary. Ask away, Deeee...tec....tive."

Tara ignored his jab. "You and your agents would have the opportunity to see every piece of art and jewelry in your client's home when you showed them to potential clients. You have keys to the homes for an easy show. Tell me, do you still have the key to the home you sold to the

Chambers after you closed the deal two years, ago?"

"Of course, not." Chambers lost his cool for a second, enough for Tara to smile. "Let me get this straight, Detective. Are you accusing me of robbing their home and killing those two sweet people? Do I need a lawyer?"

Tara smiled. "Of course not," she mimicked. "Not yet."

* * *

Five minutes later, Dobbs drove the car onto the street and glanced at Tara. "What made you think he'd sold the home to the Chambers? It wasn't in any of the reports."

Tara shrugged. "It just hit me at that moment and it was a mere guess on my part."

Dobbs grinned. "Damn good guess. Wanna go get a beer?"

Tara glanced at her watch. Half past eight and Jake was out of town buying art for three days. "Yeah, I do. You buying?"

"Nope."

"That figures."

Dobbs grinned and headed back to the precinct to pick up her car. "I'll tell you what. If you'll drink anything I ask Bob to mix, I'll pay for your drink."

Tara crossed her arms and humphed. "I'm thirsty, not suicidal."

Dobbs slapped a hand over his heart. "You don't trust me?"

A grin appeared. "Hell, no."

CHAPTER TWENTY

Sitting in a back booth at the 'Pig Sty', a local bar where the cops hang out after work to unwind, Tara took a swig of her beer. The darkened bar was busy for a week night, but most of the patrons were like her and Dobbs. They needed a quiet moment to relax out of uniform after a stressful day, so the noise level was at a minimum while everyone talked to their friends. Muted TV's hung in each corner broadcasting the sports channels.

The bartender chatted to the customers as he placed drinks in front of them at the bar. Servers with a ready smile on their faces swerved and ducked around bodies while keeping the orders from the tables filled.

"I wish I'd thought to ask Masters if he'd ever heard the name Keeper. They both run with the rich and not so famous. He could even be the Keeper for all we know. If we can believe this Teach, Keeper is linked to the Chambers and we know Masters knew them. And, they're both slime balls in my mind," Tara said.

Dobbs laughed. "You really don't care for Masters do you? What has he ever done to you?"

"Nothing. I just want to slap that contempt and disdain from his eyes every time he looks at me. I think he hates women. I didn't see him looking at you that way."

Dobbs grinned. "He's not that brave, believe me. But, you may actually have a point about them knowing each other," he pondered. "We've already decided the Keeper is raking in enough money from his illegal business to want to flaunt it with expensive things. I see him wanting to mingle with the movers and shakers in New York and possibly beyond. He's playing big time, now. Too good to be living in the alleys any longer. Problem is, we don't know what he looks like to describe him to the ones who attended the party. And, his new, rich friends wouldn't know him by the name Keeper. He may have even had the gall to give them his real name, thinking he was out of reach of the law."

"But, he would have to have a ready answer if anyone asked him what business he was in. What about Masters? Do you think he may be the Keeper? The real estate business could be a front."

"We can have his and his other agent's financials and licenses pulled to see if it's legit. But, that wouldn't tell us if he's involved in human trafficking on the side. But, let's not get tunnel vision and focus only on Masters."

Tara had to agree. The Senator's sad face from earlier repeatedly replayed across her mind. "I know. I want to catch those murderers so bad I can taste it."

Dobbs swirled his beer bottle on the moisture accumulated on the table top. "Bringing back bad memories, huh?"

Tara glanced up at Dobbs. He was one of only a handful who knew about her parent's murder by a strung out drug addict. It wasn't something she broadcasted.

She glanced back down at her beer. A hard lump formed in her throat and she drowned it down with a long drink, finishing off her beer. She waited until Dobbs ordered another round before answering.

She shook her head in wonder. "You know, it's been twenty years since it happened, but times like this makes it seem like yesterday. Watching the pain in the Senator's eyes today reminded me exactly how I felt when I lost my parents. Even though he's much older than the eight years old I was at the time, we share the same emotions."

"It's only natural that you feel a common bond with him."

Tara shrugged and looked down at her hands and continued. "I guess the Chambers death brought about feelings I can't seem to bury. I never thought I would be so emotional this many years later. I hate it."

Dobbs waited until the server brought their drinks. Compassion showed in his eyes. He leaned forward. "Tara, you've got to quit beating yourself up every time you feel sadness over your parent's death. It's only natural and as long as you're a Detective, you'll have cases like this coming up. You loved them and they were taken away from you at an early age. You will never get over that. It may mellow over time, but never go away."

Tara's nails bit into her palm. "Dobbs, it has to. How can I do my job if I can't stay neutral and unbiased?"

Dobbs took a drink and sat back, one arm casually laying across the back of the seat. "In the two years we've been partners, I've never seen you let any of this affect how you perform your job. You're too professional to let it take over your life or career. Don't sweat it, Kid. I won't let you do any less. Now. let's talk about something happier."

"Then, I guess your love life is off the table. It's pretty sad." She said this as Dobbs took a drink and beer spewed out of his mouth going across the table almost spraying her. She laughed out loud, her mood improving thanks to Dobbs.

Getting his breath back, Dobbs wiped the liquid off his face. "Thanks a lot. Even though I agree, you don't have to rub it in."

Tara nodded. "Yes. I do. I enjoy it."

Dobbs' brows narrowed. "Must I remind you that even though you have good ol' Jake in your life, your bed will be just as empty as mine tonight."

Damn. He was right.

CHAPTER TWENTY-ONE

At four a.m. Thursday morning, fifteen year old Juoinus Jackson grabbed her small carry-on and stepped off the Greyhound bus. She glanced around and a slight shiver ran down her spine. For the first time in two days, she was uncertain. But, determined.

As well as being young and alone, her tall, thin stature, well-developed breasts, dark skin showing off her white, straight teeth and multiple silver piercings drew attention from the other passengers unloading.

She barely noticed as her stomach grumbled. She'd ate one package of peanut butter crackers since she'd ran away from her home in Austin, Texas forty-eight hours before. She'd stolen enough money from her mother to buy a two way ticket to New York and forty dollars in cash to spare. She couldn't waste it on food.

Thinking of her mother, her heart saddened. Her single mother worked two jobs to support them. She worked hard for that money and Juoinus vowed she would pay her back one way or another.

Even though she'd left her a note explaining where she was going, she knew her mother would be worried by now. But, Juoinus felt driven to find her father who abandoned her and her mother when she was only four years old. She needed answers.

She would never get over her insecurities if she never confronted her father. Even at an early age she'd still remembered his smell, his smile, his laughter. She'd blamed her mother at first for her dad leaving them. And, then herself. But now, she realized he could've been part of her life if he'd wanted.

But, he hadn't.

She wanted...no, she needed to know what it was about her that her own father couldn't love.

She'd started searching for him a year ago and found him in Manhattan, with another wife, another daughter, another life.

The ones he could love.

Juoinus intentionally kept her phone turned off while she was traveling not wanting to talk to her mother just yet. Now, she turned it on. Ten frantic messages from her mother showed up. She quickly texted her to let her know she'd made it safely and then turned it back off again. She would call her after she talked to her dad.

A hand cupped her elbow drawing her out of her anguished thoughts. She jumped, fear rushed to her heart. A white man, looking to be in his thirties, with dark hair, wearing a suit, gold watch and black loafers removed his hand and smiled down at her. "I'm sorry. I didn't mean to startle you. I heard your stomach growling just then and noticed you were alone. My wife and daughter would be very upset with me if I didn't ask you if you had enough money to buy yourself breakfast and offer to buy if you don't."

Shaken, Juoinus stepped back with a timid smile and looked around. The thoughts of her mother had caused her to forget about her unfamiliar surroundings. All of the other passengers and driver had gone inside the well-lit station leaving her alone with this stranger. Dim outside lights cast an eerie silhouette over the doorway. She glanced back. With a trembling hand, she pushed her hair behind her ears and quietly answered. "Yes. I have money and my Dad will be here soon to pick me up," she lied and started for the double glass doors to the station.

The man stepped forward and opened the door for her. He followed her inside. Too close. "Well, at least let me buy you a Coke or something while you wait."

She glanced back at him. Even as her stomach grumbled again, she shook her head. "Thank you, but no. I'm fine. Excuse me." Caution overruled hunger. Without glancing his way, she headed to the restroom across the near empty station with only a couple of stragglers left waiting on their rides.

Even though he looked like the harmless family man he claimed to be, he was still a stranger who unnerved her and she wasn't taking any chances. She took her time washing up at the sink. She reapplied her make-up, checked her hair and smoothed her wrinkled blouse and jeans wanting to be presentable when she met her dad for the first time in years. She wanted him to be proud of her. To love her.

Thirty minutes later, she left the restroom and glanced around the room. The man was gone. Relieved, she opened her purse and pulled out the sheet of paper with her dad's address on it. She knew it by heart, but holding the paper in her hands made it seem more real.

Stepping out of the station, she looked around for a taxi, but they'd already left with their passengers. Juoinus looked up at the darkened sky lit by neon and sighed. Swinging her bag and purse over her shoulder, she began walking. Two blocks later she saw a taxi another block away. Exhausted, she walked faster, almost into a run, praying she could hail it before it drove away.

A large SUV sat parallel in a parking space on the side of the road. She hurried around it to get to the cab just as the door opened and hands reached out, grabbed her and shoved her into the back seat.

Screaming and thrashing, she opened her eyes and saw the man from the station. She panicked. Her heart raced.

"God, help me."

He quickly bound her hands and legs, then taped her mouth. Finished, he locked the door behind him. As he slid into the driver's seat and started the car, she tried shouting through clamped lips for help, but no one was around at that time of morning to hear her muffled screams.

The man looked at her through his rearview mirror, an evil smile now on his devilish face. "The Keepers gonna love you."

CHAPTER TWENTY-TWO

A semi-truck packed tight with concealed precious cargo drove away from a secluded warehouse under the cover of darkness. The Keeper was pleased.

*** * ***

8:00 a.m. Thursday morning, Tara and Dobbs hoped to catch Larry and Kay Brightons at home before the middle-age couple left for the day.

Tara stepped out of Dobbs' car that he'd parked on the circular drive. Stepping up onto the sidewalk, she glanced around at the manicured lawn, lush, green and floral. The three-story, dark, red brick home was edged with white trimming around the wide windows on both sides of the entrance. A large wreath with bright summer silk flowers and yellow ribbon adorned the white double front doors. Nice. All they needed was a white picket fence to make it an all American dream home.

Walking up the steps, Dobbs rang the doorbell and they waited. A moment later an elderly housekeeper in a black uniform dress opened the door and led them inside.

Tara noticed several doors led off of the large opened foyer with high ceilings as they were taken to meet the couple. She glanced into one large room as they passed. It looked like the family room. Large paintings and a family portrait hung on cheerful blue walls. The furniture and decor looked upscale, but lived in. A white winding staircase led up to the second and third floor balconies.

They followed the housekeeper into the dining area where the couple and their two young daughters were finishing breakfast. From the police reports, Tara knew the dimply, dark-haired girls were age six and eight years old. They both were a miniature to their mom with the same dark, wavy hair and blue eyes. They sat up straight when they saw the two strangers enter.

"Detective Woods and Detective Dobbs are here to see you," the housekeeper announced.

Larry Brightons, a slender man with sandy hair and nice enough facial features, if you liked granite, stood. "Please, have a seat. Mary, can you get the detectives coffee? Detectives, would you like something to eat?"

"No. Coffee would be great, though. Thank you," Tara answered. She desperately needed the strong liquid this morning after another late night.

When Mary brought the coffee and placed it in front of them, Kay Brightons asked the housekeeper to take their daughters to their rooms away from the conversation unsuited for their young ears. Larry waited until they left the room before turning back to the detectives. "So, what can we help you with? I believe we've already told the other officers everything we know."

Dobbs opened his notebook tablet and eyed the husband. "We just have a few more questions that weren't covered in the initial interviews to help us clear up a few things. I've noted that you mentioned to our officers you're a CEO with a major construction firm based in New York. You deal in malls, shopping centers and large construction sites all over the United States and beyond."

Brightons nodded. "Yes. That's correct. We have several working sites across the U.S. and other foreign countries. Asia, Singapore, Japan, Mexico to name a few."

"Do you travel often to these countries?"

Larry checked his watch and sighed. "Yes. I do. Detectives, I don't want to sound rude, but what does my job have to do with the Chambers' murder? That is why you're here, isn't it?"

Ignoring the question, Dobbs turned to Kay Brightons. "And, do you travel with him on his business trips?"

She shook her head and glanced at her husband. "No. I stay home with our daughters. They're into several school activities and don't want to miss out being with their many friends."

Dobbs typed on the keypad. He turned back to Larry. "You two hosted a party last Saturday night and the Chambers were your guests. Is that correct?"

A slight jerk of his lips showed his irritation. "Yes. They were. Look, as I mentioned, we've already gone over all of this twice before with the other officers. If there's nothing else, I'm late for a meeting."

Dobbs fingers stilled over the keypad. "Sure. It's up to you. You can either answer our questions now or later at headquarters."

"It would take up less of your time as well as ours if we finish up now, Mr. Brightons," Tara told him. She was beginning to get an inferior complex. No one wanted to talk to them about their case.

Larry pushed his coffee cup back and crossed his arms across his chest. "Fine. What else do you need to know? Let's get this over with."

Tara leaned forward and rested her crossed arms on the table. "I noticed when passing your family room and seeing the beautiful paintings on your wall, the two of you and the Chambers have the love of art in common. Did you frequent the same galleries, know the same dealers?"

He glanced at his wife and back to Tara with a tight-lipped smile. "Yes. That's how we met. Same for all of our other guests. I guess you could say we're all nerdy when it comes to fine art."

Tara leaned back in her seat and smiled. "Let me ask you this Mr. Brightons. Did you or your wife desire the Chambers paintings?"

Larry uncrossed his arms and leaned forward staring her in the eyes, undeterred. "There were a couple we would've loved to own. I offered a generous amount for them, but Bob and Edna wouldn't sell. I can't say I blame them. They were beautiful pieces."

"Did you love them enough to steal them and murder your friends to get them?" Tara sat back with a challenging smile.

Larry stood with an abruptness that caused the dining table to scoot forward. His teeth clenched. His hands fisted by his side. "No. I did not. Now, you can either officially charge me for the theft and murder or you can get the hell out of my home. I've had enough. Contact my lawyer from now on."

Dobbs stood with a deceptive slowness and nodded. "We will, but let me clue you in on something, Brightons. I'm very easy to get along with. But, if you'd touched Detective Woods with the table you shoved toward her, you'd need more than your lawyer. I'd slapped charges on you so fast it would make your head swim for assaulting an officer. Believe me, you don't want to ever make that mistake with me, again." They turned and walked out after the smirk faded from Larry Brightons' face.

* * *

Back at headquarters an hour later, Tara stood in front of the crime board in her office. Her fingers itched to move the pictures of the Brightons couple closer to the victims as their main suspects. But, she hesitated and glanced back at Dobbs. His feet were propped on top of her desk as he thumbed through the notes he'd made on his tablet.

She turned back to her board and spoke her thoughts out loud. "I don't know if I can believe it's a coincidence that Brightons' job takes him several times a year to countries well known for endless human trafficking."

Dobbs cocked an eyebrow toward her. "Foolish me. I thought we were interviewing him as a suspect in a robbery and murder case. Next you'll be telling me that Brightons, a family man with a wife and two daughters is the Keeper and has Annie." Dobbs laughed and went back to reading his notes.

His gaze flew back up at Tara when he realized she wasn't laughing. His feet shot off the desk and he stood. "My God. You do think he may be the Keeper. Are you serious? I know we talked about the connection, but you can't believe Brightons is the Keeper. "

Tara shrugged and scowled. "He fits the description. He's rich, moves in upper class circles, knows the most influential people of New York. He travels to foreign countries. Plus, may I point out that these are foreign countries that is notorious for white slavery. And, his wife seemed clueless. She's too busy playing housewife and mother to pay attention to what her husband is doing."

"That fits the description of about one hundred thousand other men and women in New York."

"But, those men or women weren't aware the Chambers would be at the party Saturday night leaving their home empty. The Teach said if we found the Keeper, we'd have the ones who killed and robbed the Chambers and we'd find Annie."

"Oh, yeah. The Teach. He sounds like someone we can really trust."

"Stuff it, Dobbs. Do you have any better ideas?"

Dobbs ran his hands through his hair and sighed. "No. The stolen paintings would be worth a lot of money on the black market. And, I'll be the first to admit I know very little about contemporary art, but the paintings I saw in the Brightons' home looked a lot more expensive than the Chambers and looked just as good on their walls. And, did you see the bling on Kay Brightons' hands? Fort Knox on her fingers."

Tara glanced down at her ring less fingers. "I don't understand why someone would want to wear that many expensive rings at one time. Evidently, she's never tried to do a pat search on anyone. Those rings could do some damage."

Dobbs grinned and shook his head. "Only you would think that. But, back to what we were discussing, looking at the Brightons' bank records, they don't need to steal to live the good life. His job provides them with enough money." Dobbs sat back down and rubbed his eyes. "This case is about to frustrate the crap out of me. Every time we get a new lead, I think we have something huge we can work with to solve the murder. But, then it shrivels up to nothing and the hours are ticking away. At this point, I'm ready to use anything or anybody. Even the Teach."

"Frustrating? Something huge···then, shrivels up? Are you talking about your sex prowess or this case?" Her eyes sparkled. Sometimes she needed to lighten up their moods, or the stress would get to them.

Dobbs' eyes narrowed to slits. He rose from his chair and took a step forward leaning over her desk. He looked down into her mischievous eyes and grinned. He said. "Aaaahhh, now you're questioning my performance. Want me to show you how non-shriveled my ⋯ummm, sex prowess is?"

Tara took a quick step back, ducked under his arm and said, "No, thank you. We've got a case to solve." She swept out of her office with a grin. His laughter followed her down the hallway.

God, she loved jerking his chain. And, she did what she'd set out to do. She'd made him laugh.

CHAPTER TWENTY-THREE

Two o'clock Thursday afternoon, Chief Haynes summoned Tara and Dobbs to his office. When they arrived a few minutes later, a man and woman looking to be in their mid-forties sat in his office. The dark-haired woman wrung her hands, her face blotchy from the tears streaming down her face. The man, graying at the temples had his arm wrapped around her. They both looked past exhaustion, surviving on nervous adrenalin, Tara thought.

Chief Haynes introduced them. "This is Mr. and Mrs. Reynolds. They are looking for their daughter, Annie."

Tara gave the couple a sharp glance. "Our Annie?"

The Chief answered. "Same name. Yes, we believe so."

Mr. Reynolds spoke up. "Detectives, the police department in our home town, Bowling Green, Kentucky told us you were inquiring about our daughter. We flew here as soon as we could get a flight. Do you think she may be in New York? Have you seen her? Do you know where she is?" His hopeful gaze swept from Tara to

Dobbs as the questions shot out of his mouth at rapid speed.

Tara opened up her cell phone and pulled up the picture she had of Annie. "First, let me make sure we're talking about the same girl. Is this your daughter?" She showed the picture to the couple.

The woman's hand went to her mouth and she sobbed out. "Oh my god. It's her. Yes, look honey, it's Annie. Is she okay?" Hope filled her eyes.

Tara answered with caution, choosing her words with a gentle care. "I'm sorry, but we haven't seen her. We do, however, have reason to believe she was in New York two days, ago. She was seen then. But, she disappeared once again. Mr. and Mrs. Reynolds, I wish I had better news to tell you."

The father's shoulders sagged. Fresh tears ran down his wife's worn face. He sighed clearly fighting his own tears. "Thank God for that. Sweetheart, at least we know she was alive, then. It's more than we knew before. We've been worried out of our minds these past months. We went back home Sunday after looking for her all weekend. We've been desperate to find her."

"Yes. Thank God. Was she well? How was she?" the mother asked, her voice desperate.

"From what we were told she was safe and well two days, ago."

"Are you still looking for our Annie?" she asked.

Dobbs smiled and squatted in front of the couple, handing them each a tissue. He answered, his voice soothing. "We don't want you to worry any more than you are, so we'll tell you what we can. It's still an ongoing investigation. But, yes, we are still looking. The problem is we're Homicide Detectives. We're limited in what we can do. Missing Persons is involved, as well. We'll be working with them to help find her."

The father shook his head. "I don't understand. If you're Homicide why would you be inquiring about a missing teen, if she's thought to be alive?"

Dobbs glanced at the Chief. With his nod of consent, Dobbs explained to the older couple. "We don't believe your daughter is involved, but the person we think she might be with right now may have robbed and murdered an elderly couple in their home Saturday night."

The wife moaned and leaned into her husband.

Mr. Reynolds pulled her closer and asked, "So, you're saying if you find the killers you might find Annie?"

"Yes, we believe so," Tara told them.

Mrs. Reynolds sucked in a breath and her hand covered her lips. "Annie would never be involved in anything like that unless she was forced into it. She's a good girl, just a little misguided. Will you help us get her back from that monster?"

"I promise you, we will do everything we can to find your daughter," Dobbs told her. He patted the woman's hand and stood.

"Can you tell us a little more about Annie? Why did she run away?" Tara asked.

"It's my fault…," The father started.

"I've told you a million times over it's not your fault, Greg. You did what any good father would have done," Annie's mother told him, patting his hand.

Before her husband could protest, she turned back to Tara and continued. "Right after the Christmas and New Year holiday this year, Annie was in her Freshmen year. She turned sixteen a few days after school started back after the holidays. That's when we noticed her whole demeanor changed. She began staying out late, dressing more provocative and she became argumentative with us all the time."

Mr. Reynolds continued. "She became sullen and moody, her good grades in school dropped, the friends she used to hang out with quit coming over."

Annie's mother nodded. "She didn't mention their names anymore. We tried talking to her, to find out what was wrong, but she wouldn't talk to us. Then, her principle called and asked if we could meet with her. That's when we found out Annie had started hanging out with a new guy at school. He'd just been transferred to her school about a month before. As the Principle said, the boy was bad news and she was worried about Annie. He was truant at least a couple days a week, starting fights in school and his grades were failing. His parents neglected him and he did whatever he wanted. The Principle suspected drugs might be involved, but he had never been caught with anything. I couldn't believe what I was hearing. Annie had always been so sweet and loving. Like I said, she was a good girl. She always came to us with her problems. She knew she could talk to us. But, she kept this boy a secret from us."

"That's when I forbid her to see him, again." The father took over explaining. "We had a huge fight that night. She was in love, she said. We couldn't stop her from seeing him. Then, she stormed up to her room and that's the last time we saw her. She left in the middle of the night along with a suitcase and about two hundred dollars taken from her savings she kept in her room."

"What about the boy? Is he missing, as well?" Dobbs asked.

"He was, but he returned two days later and said the two of them had gotten into a fight and he'd left her at the hotel room close to West

Virginia and came home. The police checked all of the camera's around the four block area of the hotel and he did leave without her. His mother's stolen credit card was used after that at a couple gas stations, a McDonalds and a video store showing the timeline of all purchases as he drove home. The hotel camera showed her leaving about two hours after him walking with her suitcase toward the bus station where she'd bought a ticket to New York. The New York Greyhound bus station camera showed her leaving the bus and walking into the station. The police lost her trail from there. They contacted other stations in the surrounding areas, but she was never seen on camera or anywhere else, again. We've had no other leads to go on, until now. And, believe me, we've looked. I just don't understand why she didn't come home. She know we would've forgiven her."

Tara's heart melted. Annie was just a misguided teen with loving parents who fell for the wrong guy. The one and only time she defied her parents landed her in a bucket full of trouble. "Do you have a better picture of her we can have?" They had the one off of the computer, but it was grainy.

"Yes. We have these posters we had made to hang all over our town. We thought we would hang up some here in New York if it's allowed. You can have one of these. It has her latest picture on it." The mother reached beside the chair and handed them a rolled up 16" X 20" poster with all of the girl's information along with her picture.

"Thank you. Will you be staying in New York for a while?" Chief Haynes asked.

The father shook his head. "I have to get back to work or I'll lose my job. We've spent all of our savings on trying to find Annie. But, we'll be back this weekend. Can we call you for updates?"

"Absolutely." Tara told them. They exchange cell phone numbers.

"Mr. and Mrs. Reynolds, we'll do everything we can to help Missing Persons find your daughter and bring her home to you. I promise," Tara told them.

Mrs. Reynolds teared up, again. "Thank you. I can't eat. I can't sleep and the same for Greg. He's worn to a frazzle. We've got to find Annie. We just have to."

* * *

Teach's students were getting restless. They wanted to make a hit and they wanted to find Annie.

A hit was out of the question for now. Cops and the two detectives were swarming all over the case. Even though, he didn't believe in awarding failure, he believed his students had learned their lesson from the last fiasco. But, he couldn't take the chance. Organizing a hit this soon after the murder only asked for trouble.

They would lay low for a while, but that didn't mean he wouldn't keep them busy looking for Annie. Each boy had his own special skill to use in the search. He had taught them well.

Now, it was time to test them.

Teach walked out of his office and walked down the long hall. He found his students lounging around the plush family room. Gator sat on one end of the white, soft leather couch with his feet propped on the coffee table. He was playing a game on his phone. BoneZ sat on a recliner leaned back and snoring. Striker and Cruiser were watching a show about restoring old cars on the 60" screen T.V. hanging on the wall. Three boys glanced up for a second as Teach walked into the room. They greeted him with a "Hey, Teach.", then they went back to what they were doing.

Teach grabbed the remote and turned the TV off. He took the phone out of Gator's hand and slapped his feet off the table. With one swift movement, he grabbed the handle of the recliner shooting the foot rest down and BoneZ flew forward waking him. "Hey, what the hell?" BoneZ cursed.

Teach walked to the center of the room and faced his students. "Listen up, boys. Today, we're going on a class trip."

"Where're we goin', Teach?" Striker asked.

"Back to our past, boys. Back to our past."

The four boys looked at each other with raised brows, then back at Teach. "You been smokin' dope, Teach?" BoneZ asked.

Teach grinned. "No, BoneZ, I haven't. What I meant by us going back to our past is that we're going back to the same streets and alleys we lived on before I moved you into this home. We're going to revert back to the skills we had to master to survive on those streets. Before you guys went soft on me. We're going to find Annie."

Huge smiles and the four boys started talking at once.

Teach held out his hand to quiet them. "Listen up, boys. We have a lot of area to cover tonight. So, when we hit the streets I want each of you to split up and look up the old contacts you had back then. Even if they've moved on, find them. They may still hear things. Chat up any new faces you see. Throw the name Keeper out there, see what, if anything is being said about him. See if there are any whispers about human trafficking increasing recently. And, take a picture of Annie with you to show. Maybe someone you asked yesterday may have seen her today. Ask if they've noticed anybody else missing. Any questions, Students?"

"Nah. We know what to do, Teach. When are we leaving?" Gator asked.

Teach grinned. "As soon as you put on your dirty, alley face and clothes, we'll leave."

"Aaaah, man. I don't miss that part at all," Cruiser moaned.

"Suck it up, boys. And, remember my rules. Blend in, move fast and always stay safe. You won't be able to work in pairs this time. So, I want to hear from each of you every hour on the hour. If you don't call, I'll know something is wrong and we'll come looking. If you get in trouble, sneak your hand into your pocket and speed dial me and stay silent. I'll track you down that way. Anything else?"

"No, Mother. We're big boys. We'll be fine," Stricker mocked.

Teach grinned and swatted at Striker's head. Stricker laughed and stepped back.

"Okay, boys. Let's get a move on." Teach led the way out of the room.

CHAPTER TWENTY-FOUR

Tara and Dobbs left Chief Haynes's office. More calls were coming in about missing teens. The latest was of a runaway girl leaving her mother in Austin, Texas to see her estranged father in New York.

The girl never made it.

Missing Persons was working the case after the mother had contacted the father. He then reported his daughter missing in New York. They thought Tara and Dobbs would be interested in this latest case.

With the new information racing through her mind, Tara slid behind the wheel, buckled up and started the car. She glanced over at Dobbs.

"Sounds like the Keeper is turning into a very busy man."

Dobbs leaned back against the head rest. He pinched his bottom lip and stared out of the side window for a few seconds. He glanced her way. "We don't know for sure if this is the Keeper's work. We only have the Teachers word that Keeper exists."

Tara shrugged and pulled out of the parking lot. "True. But, I would bet a week's paycheck that he does exist and it is The Keeper. And, no I don't trust the Teacher as far as I can throw him. But, what he told us about the missing Annie is true. The Teacher may be as crooked as the day is long, but he wants to find Annie as much as we and her parents do. So, in that aspect, we have to trust him on this Keeper."

"Maybe." Dobbs went back to staring out the window. They rode in silence for long minutes, both deep in their own thoughts.

A few side roads later, Dobbs glanced back at Tara. "You know, with your hair in a ponytail and no makeup on your face, you look about sixteen."

Tara gave him a sharp glance. Her eyes narrowed. "Are you dissing me?"

Dobbs roared with laughter. "Does anyone ever say that anymore? Dissing? For real?"

Tara growled beneath her breath. "Now, you're pissing me off. And, I know that's a word." She slapped at his arm.

Dobbs laughed harder. At her penetrating glare, he finally sputtered, "What I was trying to say is if we went undercover, we might get more answers than questions from the kids off the street."

"Ahhhh, I get it. You want me to play a little girl and you would be my Pimp. God, Dobbs. You're getting kinky in your old age."

Dobbs grinned and did the Groucho Marx brows before turning serious. "Actually, I was thinking of a younger sister of Annie's. They may be sympathetic enough to talk to a sibling of a missing girl. So, what do you think?"

"Sounds good to me. We don't have any other leads to follow up on, right now. But, it will be dark in a couple of hours. Why don't we make a swing by our apartments and change clothes. That should give us plenty of time to check out several areas in the city before dinner time. And, you're buying."

An hour later, the two were hitting the streets. Both were dressed in jeans, t-shirts and running shoes. Tara, as Dobbs suggested had scrubbed her face clean and her hair was pulled back in a ponytail. Her jeans and t-shirt fit tight against her curves. Dobbs had his t-shirt sleeve pulled up so that his snake tattoo and muscles showed and he wore one silver earring in his ear.

Tara decided to park her car in a safer neighborhood, so they walked four blocks over to a different world. Trash littered the streets. Rusty, abandoned cars with tires missing and hoods raised were jacked up all along the curbs. Houses and apartments sat side by side, all with peeling white paint, windows broken and most of the doors off the hinges. Several men, women or teens sat on doorsteps looking as damaged and abandoned and as high as the jacked up cars sitting in front of their homes.

One thin man with gray, stringy hair and what looked like a month's growth of facial hair, wearing a dingy muscle shirt and cotton shorts held a bottle of whiskey in one hand and a cigarette in the other. He showed them a toothless smile as they walked toward him looking young and harmless.

Tara cringed and stopped in front of the man. She showed the picture of Annie that her parent's had given them. "Hi. I was hoping you could help me find my sister. She's a runaway. Have you seen her around here?" The man licked his lips as he looked Tara up and down. He burped loudly and slurred, "Naw, but if she looks as pretty as you, young thang, I hope I do."

Dobbs took a step forward until he was right behind her. Tara forced a grin. "Thank you, sir. If you do see her, can you call this number? We would appreciate your help." Tara handed the man a phone number written on a post it. They turned and left.

The neighborhood only got worse the further they went. Gangs in their bright colors with knives in full view lined certain streets. Each had their own areas they commanded and no other gangs had the right or nerve to step into an enemies' territory. Unless, they were willing to die. Tara hated to admit it, but even the police patrols with their issued weapons hated to drive these streets. It took a tough cop with no fear of dying for the job they were hired to do.

An hour later, after showing Annie's picture around and getting propositioned by gang members and pipe heads, they were no better off. Everyone was too jittery, too drunk, too high or too lazy or mean to talk to them.

Walking back to the car, they decided they would take a short dinner break and head back to the office. Tara's hands unclenched for the first time in an hour. Now, she remembered why she'd sought the Detective badge after months of street patrol. Even though lately, her Detective life hadn't been that much safer.

Tara glanced at her watch. 7:00 p.m. on the dot. "I say we eat a bite and call it a night. We're exhausted and we'll have clearer minds in the morning."

Dobbs nodded and rubbed the back of his calf. "Sounds like a plan. I think we're both exhausted enough that we'll sleep good tonight."

* * *

Friday morning, Dobbs replaced the phone receiver and growled deep in his throat. "I have no life," he complained to an empty room and then Tara walked into his office.

"No life as in no love life?" she asked as she sat across from him.

"Both. Do you realize neither one of us have taken a vacation in over a year? We've had one day off in three weeks. I've had one date in three weeks. And, I just had to turn down a date for tonight because of this case. Tara," he moaned. "I need to stare into a woman's eyes instead of that dang crime board."

"What am I, Swiss cheese? The last time I looked into the mirror, I was a woman." Tara propped her feet on his desk and grinned.

Dobbs eyed her up and down. "Oh yeah. You are definitely a woman, but if I stared into your eyes like a lover you'd punch me in the gut or Jake would. You don't count unless you're getting rid of Jake."

Tara snorted. "Not on your life. But Jake has been gone for two days on this buying trip. So, I know what you mean. I'm lonely, too. When this case is over we need to get away for a while before we burn out. I'm thinking a cruise or a condo on a beach. Find yourself a date and we'll make it a foursome." Tara smiled at the thought of getting away.

Then, Dobbs' phone rang. The thought of paradise vanished as they heard Chief Haynes on the phone.

CHAPTER TWENTY-FIVE

During the darkness of night, this corrupt section of the city came alive with riff-raff, drunks, druggies and murderers.

Party-goers walking out of the seedy nightclubs or greasy burger joints laughed, fought, stumbled and weaved or made out beneath the garish, flickering neon lights between the buildings. A drunk elderly man in a dark business suit leaned against a graffiti wall emptying his liquid-filled bladder oblivious of any loved ones who he might have waiting and worrying at home.

Drug dealers and hookers standing on the street corners didn't bother to watch behind their backs as they traded their goods for money out in the open. They didn't care. The large amount of money that changed hands was worth the slight slap on the wrists by any cop who made a round or two into their underworld. The drug dealers snitched for a lesser cell time and being thrown in jail was a weekly spa vacation for the hookers.

Homeless people with fires blazing in oil drums to warm the night chill and sleeping on the ground beneath cardboard enclosures settled down for the night on empty stomachs and abandoned hope. They witnessed coldblooded acts of relentless murders, rapes and children being snatched right before their eyes. But, they knew to keep their mouths shut and heads turned. Or, they would be next.

Yes. The night was when the evil set in Striker decided while standing in the shadows taking in the familiar sights before him. Damn, he'd become too used to the finer things in life, he thought as he sidestepped a dumpster and mud puddle to avoid the filth getting on his old, familiar jeans and boots.

Striker, Gator, Cajun and BoneZ had split up an hour before and combed the New York City's back alleys and neighboring boroughs looking for Annie and this Keeper. Recognizable faces from his own desperate days on the streets, before the Teach took him in, either welcomed him back or exhibited fear and hurried away.

Striker was aware the four's past on the streets were well-known by their peers and their legend had been passed on to the newer additions of runaways. The Teach and his students were respected and feared. And, rightly so.

But, right now the fear was working against him. No one wanted to be seen talking or snitching. But, he was determined and with a relentless brusqueness he questioned or threatened strangers and everyone he knew who could help them find Annie.

To no avail.

It seemed they feared the Keeper more than him.

Striker moved even deeper into the darkness and hoped the other three were having better luck than him.

***

At 4:00 A.M. Friday morning, Teach summoned them home.

As soon as they arrived, one after another, the Teach called a meeting. Exhausted, the four entered the living room and plopped down on the couch and recliners, preferring to climb out of their stinking clothes and crash onto their beds and sleep for days. But, first things first. They needed to report and compare their findings.

Striker rubbed his red eyes and yawned. He glanced at the Teach and shrugged. "I've got nothing. If anyone's seen Annie, they're not talking."

"Same here," BoneZ added. "But, when I mentioned the name Keeper, Lord, you'd think I'd said the 'Reaper' the way they acted. Scared shitless, man. They either rushed away or warned me away. And, something else I noticed. All night long, I only met two different teens hunkered down for the night and they both said they'd gotten there a few hours before, fresh off the Greyhound. It was like a teen ghost town, man. "

The other boys nodded their heads and agreed with BoneZ. The night had been the same for them, they told Teach. Even their trusted allies from their pasts had warned them to tread lightly. Living off the streets wasn't easy and downright dangerous at any given time, but now it was even more so, it seemed.

Sinister.

A feeling they couldn't easily shrug off, they told him.

The Teach paced the floor. He rubbed his chin while he thought about what his students revealed. More than not finding Annie, more than the wasted hours on the streets and, more than the missing teens unnerved him. It seemed like his hard earned authority in his kingdom was being usurped by The Keeper.

His lips curled into a snarl. He wasn't quite ready to give up what he'd fought so hard to obtain, though. No one, especially that lowlife wannabe would ever knock him off his throne. It was time to remind everyone on the streets who they truly needed to fear.

A weary smirk appeared. He hadn't earned the name Teach for no reason. A much needed lesson was about to be delivered.

The Teach rubbed his tired eyes. He hadn't slept himself. He'd been busy contacting his own sources of political officials asking them delicate questions no one else would dare to ask. It was a risky chance he took if he asked the wrong questions to the wrong people. But, he still believed the Keeper was someone with a lot of clout in the City. He had a feeling the people off the streets weren't the only one who feared him.

One name had been scratched off his list to question, though.

Senator Chambers, the son of the couple his students murdered. Not that he felt guilty or remorse for their deaths. Or, not much. He just didn't trust the Senator as far as he could throw him. He'd never liked the man when he'd met him at random parties or other social functions. Beneath the fake smile, his arctic eyes gave him away. Teach never did put much trust into politicians.

But, the Teach had other ways to find out more about the dirt on the Senator without giving away his hand or alerting the man's security network system. He loved a good challenge.

He grinned and turned back to his students. "Good job, Students. Let's call it a night and start fresh later today. Don't worry. We'll bring little Annie home."

* * *

Tara and Dobbs sat across from each other in a booth at a local café down from the Police Station. Tara stared down into her third cup of black coffee.

Connie, a waitress at least twice his age flirted easily with Dobbs as she did every morning while waiting on them. She poured his coffee and then cleared the empty breakfast plates from their table before moving to another table where a young couple sat.

Normally, Tara would tease Dobbs about being desperate enough to flirt with anyone in skirts, but this morning her mind was occupied with their case. She sighed and took a sip of her fresh coffee, instead.

Dobbs wiped his mouth and laid the napkin on the table. With a deceiving innocent glance her way, he ran the side of his booted foot lightly up her pants leg. He grinned when she snarled and moved her leg away. "Finally, I have your attention. What's got your g-string in a knot this morning?" he asked with a teasing glint in his eyes. "You haven't said two words to me all morning and you passed up the chance to tease me about Connie. That's not like you. Are you sick or just missing Jake?"

Tara pushed her coffee cup away and searched for tip money in her pocket. "It's nothing," she said, still distracted.

"Hey, I know you too well for that bull crap, Partner. Something's bothering you. I'm here if you want to talk."

She met his gaze and a genuine smile appeared. She placed her hand on top of his and simply said, "I know. I'm sorry I was bad company. I had my mind on our case. Something keeps nagging my brain and I can't figure out what it is." She threw some money on the table and stood. "Let's get to work, Partner. Unless, you want to take Connie up on her flirty offer while paying our bill. I'll wait for you in the car."

Minutes later, Dobbs started the car, turned the air on high and glanced over at Tara. "So, you want to talk it through, maybe bounce what we know so far back and forth to see if anything pops out at us?"

Tara shrugged and fiddled with the radio knob, finally selecting a local country station. Settling back in her seat, she waited until Dobbs pulled out of the cafe parking lot before answering, "The meeting with the Chief yesterday keeps playing around in my mind. The precinct and Missing Persons have gotten so many phone calls in the last couple of days with reports of missing teens."

"I know. That's had me worried, as well. Something more than the ordinary is going on."

"I agree. And, I've been thinking about how all of our dots on the crime board run between the Chambers' murder, this missing Annie, Teach, The Keeper, the abundant amount of runaways and straight to the white slavery. I think there's too many players in this game."

A thoughtful nod from Dobbs, "I would say they should all connect. But, man, I don't see how they could. Right?"

"Right. I can't figure out how the Chambers were involved with white slavery. With everything we've learned about the couple, it doesn't add up to me. They were a pillar of the community and political arena, well-liked and they had money. But, not the kind of money a scum would earn in a white slavery market. And, I don't see them wanting to harm their only son's political career."

Dobbs turned on to their street. "I don't see them as being involved, either. More like innocent victims to me."

"And, one other thing that doesn't make sense to me. Why would The Keeper bother with a small time murder and robbery when he's making millions with his runaway teen trade?"

Dobbs parallel parked in front of the Police Station and killed the motor. They wouldn't be inside long. "You have a different theory?"

Tara shrugged, opened her door and stepped out onto the sidewalk. She turned to Dobbs when he joined her. "My gut is telling me the Teach lied to us, which isn't a big surprise. I don't think the dots from Annie, Teach, Keeper and the runaway teens connect to the Chambers at all."

"I don't believe it, either. I think it's two different cases and I still wonder how the Teach knew so much about the murder and stolen items. We never broadcasted that information to the media."

"True. I think we need to find this Teach and ask him."

Dobbs nodded and started walking in the opposite direction of their offices, his long strides taking him down the hallway. "Let's get Melinda started on checking everything she can find out about Teach. Hopefully, the name Teach will pop up somewhere on her databases. Some snitch, somewhere may have mentioned the name during some other criminal interrogation. If so, we should be able to find out his real identity and make our lives easier. We can try our snitches again, too."

Tara tried to match his stride and failed. "Hey, slow down. You're killing me."

He grinned and slowed his steps until she caught up with him.

Walking beside him now, she added, "Also, we need to talk to the Senator, again. I want to see if he can enlighten us on any possible connection between his parents and this Teach. I know it's a far reach, but he may recognize the name and be able to tell us the Teach's real name."

"Oh great. We don't stay in enough trouble as it is. Pissing the Senator off by accusing him of socializing with a thief should put us on the bus straight to the unemployment line after he calls the Chief, Mayor and the City Council members and chews their butts off. We didn't leave the Senator a happy man the last time, you know?"

Tara grinned and shrugged. "The Senator likes me, but you should be worried," she said as she entered Melinda's office. She heard a menacing growl behind her and her grin widened.

CHAPTER TWENTY-SIX

Tara gritted her teeth, a quiet curse escaped. She gently replaced the phone receiver instead of slamming it down as she wanted. She glanced up at Dobbs who had listened to her side of the phone conversation while he stared out her office window. A frown curled his lips downward.

"Chief agrees the teens are being snatched as soon as they arrive in New York, but he doesn't have any extra manpower to patrol all of the bus stations and airports around. He says it's up to us and the task force assigned to the missing teens."

Dobbs shrugged. "We knew that was coming, but it was worth a try. Call Officer Jackson. I'd like to see what he found out on the bus route this latest girl, the one traveling to see her Dad took. He should be able to find out her destination from her ticket purchase and can be pulled up on their computers. If we can find out which station she arrived at we can check the cameras."

Tara agreed. "If we know where at least one of the snatches occurred hopefully the camera will reveal one of the kidnappers and he can lead us straight to the Keeper."

"Exactly."

Tara sighed. "I left out one little part."

"What's that?"

"Chief wants us to spend our time on the Chamber's murder and robbery. Senator Chambers is putting a lot of pressure on the Mayor and the Commissioner who both are pressuring the Chief."

"Even though we haven't had enough info to rule out both cases possibly being connected?"

"Even though." Tara shrugged again. "I totally understand a person wanting to find their parents' murderer. Been there, done that and I sympathize. But, I can become a real bitch when someone in a high position demands I conduct my investigation the way they want. I don't like it."

"Yeah, same here. To hell with the Senator. Call Jackson."

Tara grinned. "You're going rogue on me, Dobbs. I like it."

* * *

Two hours later, Jackson came through for them and less than thirty minutes from then Tara and Dobbs stepped through the door of the bus station where Juoinus Jackson, the latest kidnapped victim they were aware of had last been seen.

Walking to the counter Dobbs asked for the station manager. Within minutes after introducing themselves to the friendly and eager young manager, the camera tape from the date they needed was being played for them, a simultaneous four frame picture of both the outside and inside of the station.

They immediately recognized the young girl from the picture her mother had emailed them as she stepped off the bus with her carry on. They watched the camera scene play out for them.

A Caucasian male who looked to be in his early thirties of slight build and dark hair approached the girl. They talked briefly with the girl showing hesitancy with the stranger. A few minutes later they both entered the bus station together. Moments later the girl left the man and made a trip to the bathroom with her belongings. The camera showed the man leave the station seconds later. Ten minutes later she exited the bathroom with her carry on, looked with caution around the station and then left the building alone.

Outside, she glanced around with a frightened gaze as if looking for a ride or person who hadn't showed up. Giving up, she pulled a folded sheet of paper from her purse, glanced at it for a long moment before returning it to her purse. Glancing around once more, her shoulders sagged and she began walking down the street.

Mere seconds later, the same man she had talked to when exiting the bus came out of the building and monitored the girl for a minute before walking toward the parking lot. He drove off slow in a new, grey SUV heading in the same direction as the girl. License plates unreadable from the camera and both the girl and SUV were out of view.

Dobbs held up his hand. "You can stop the tape now. I think we have our man."

"I think so, too. We would like to borrow this tape if you don't mind. Our computer analysis may be able to bring up a clearer view of the license plate and hopefully give us a name to this jerk," Tara requested.

"Not at all. Take what you need. I'll help anyway I can to take scumbags like that off the streets. Especially, if they want to turn my bus station into a crime scene."

"Thank you. We appreciate your cooperation. And, if you and your employees happen to see this guy again or anything looking strange, please give us a call." Tara handed him her business card.

"No problem. I'll let everyone know to keep their eyes out for this guy."

"Thank you." She turned to Dobbs. "Let's get this to Melinda."

* * *

The Keeper slapped Annie across the face. Her head slammed back against the metal chair and she whimpered. For once, he had brought her out of her hidden prison inside the abandoned warehouse. Her eyes were still adjusting to the bright lights of the large dirty room, but they were defiant. As always.

He would break her spirit, yet.

"Boss?"

The Keeper stepped back from the girl, tightened his silk tie around his neck and turned toward the voice.

Ben stood inside the door and the Keeper waved him inside a room once used as an office when it was a manufacturing warehouse. Ben, a giant of a man with, dark skin, cold eyes and bald head was his Chief of staff and right hand man with more than ten men working under him.

Ignoring the girl tied to a chair, the Keeper walked to his desk and sat down. The bent metal desk and torn leather chair was much different than his costly office furniture downtown. He cringed at the dirt smudging on his tailored suit.

"I have a meeting in ten minutes. What's on your mind?'

Ben shuffled his feet for a few seconds before answering. He cleared his throat, glanced at the girl and then back to the Keeper. "Boss, we have a problem. Am I allowed to talk in front of the girl?"

"Of course. She is nothing of concern. But, I believe I pay you to take care of my problems. Why are you bothering me?" The Keeper grabbed a folder off his desk and looked through it.

"You do, Boss. But, I thought you needed to know about this. One of our field guys just told me several boys are hitting the streets asking for information about The Keeper and showing pictures of her." He pointed at Annie before continuing. "From what our guy said, I don't believe they've got any information off the streets. Everyone is too scared of you to open their mouths."

The Keeper's features froze. He dropped the bulky file back on to his desk and glanced up. His voice chilled the air causing fear in the man standing before him. "Find these boys and put a stop to their questions. I don't care what you have to do to silence them. But, silence them. Get the message out that I'll take care of anyone who opens their mouths to them. Well, what are you waiting on. Do it." His raised voice caused the girl to jump and quiver. A soft moan escaped her mouth.

Ben glanced down, but didn't move to leave. "There's one other thing you should know about. A couple of detectives was snooping around on the streets."

"And?" Keeper's voice spat out as deadly and as quickly as a cobra snake.

"They were asking the same questions about you and her, just like the boys were. What do you want me to do about the detectives, Boss?"

The Keeper's temper rose and then he grinned. "Nothing, Ben. I don't want you to do anything. Leave the detectives to me."

After Ben quickly left the office, The Keeper rose and paced the floor while he thought. Then, he stopped and pulled out his cell phone and dialed. When after three rings it was picked up on the other end, he said, "Ben, I've changed my mind about the boys. I want you to find them and bring them to this warehouse. Call me when you have them." The Keeper ended the call and smiled. So, whoever was looking for him had to be working for the man who had stolen Annie from him. No one else would dare to search for him in the alleyways.

The Keeper grinned. He would make sure he was easily found. He had a major score to settle with him. No one stole his merchandise and got away with it. And, he had a feeling he knew the person the Detectives were asking questions about.   He could easily squash all of them between his palms like a couple of aggravating mosquitoes. They weren't worth another thought.

CHAPTER TWENTY–SEVEN

"Dobbs? Tara? I enlarged the bus station's camera image and got the numbers off of the SUV's license plate," Melinda said as she stepped into Tara's office. "They ran the plates. Unfortunately, they came back as coming off of a stolen rental taken from a New Jersey couple staying in a hotel nearby."

Dobbs looked up and cursed beneath his breath. "That figures. Have they found the vehicle yet? They would've dumped it by now."

"They're searching signals now. The GPS tracking should lead us to it. We should know something soon."

"Thanks Melinda. Will you keep us posted?" Tara asked. Why couldn't they ever catch a break with this case?

"Is there anything else I can do for you?"

Tara nodded. "Yes. Keep looking for any information on this Teach. Also, keep broadcasting the picture of the guy from the bus station to all of your networks. Maybe we can get lucky with him."

"Will do. I'll let you know as soon as I hear anything."

"Thanks Melinda." Dobbs turned back to Tara as soon as Melinda left. "Even if they find the vehicle they're not going to find any prints. These guys are too good to be clumsy enough to leave prints."

"I agree. We can only hope Melinda comes through for us and finds someone who knows Teach or the Keeper."

* * *

Friday night, Striker and Gator snuck out of the Penthouse without Teach's knowledge. Even though the Teach had told them to let him handle this, they had to try one more time to find Annie.

In the darkest shadows of the alley, they whispered to a young boy they knew from their days on the streets. They hadn't run into him the night before. The two filled him in on the happenings of Annie's kidnapping.

Petey, the gaunt, dark-headed boy of seventeen glanced around. His sharp gaze took in the whole length of the alleyway in a survival mode while he talked. "The Keeper is scary as shit, man." He held up two fingers almost touching. "I came this close to being snatched by his goons yesterday. But, this boy ain't stupid. I know these streets better than those idiots. I kicked one hard enough that he'll never breed and then I ran like the devil was on my heels. I have too many hiding places for them to find me. But, I'm telling you it scared the crap out of me. Word is out that his goons have been crisscrossing the streets all night looking for you guys. We need to stick together and eliminate this Keeper. He's pickin' us youngin's off one at a time."

Striker and Gator agreed. Something had to be done. They'd finally found someone willing to talk who might help them. "Have you ever heard anyone mention if they know who this Keeper's real name is?" Striker asked.

Petey nodded. "I've heard rumors. I don't know if it's true or not. If it is, stopping him will be like knocking down a mile long brick wall with your fist. Impossible."

"Nothing is impossible. For Annie and the other missing teens, we have to stop him," Gator reminded him.

"What name have you heard?" Striker asked.

When Petey gave the name, Striker moaned. "You can't be serious?"

Petey shrugged. "Just tellin' you what I heard."

"And, it's a big help. This is going to be tougher than we thought. Have you ever heard the name Teach?" Striker asked.

"Yeah, everyone on the streets has heard about him. Heard he's an okay guy, and always there if you need him, unless you get on his bad side. Then, you'd better run like hell and hide. I heard you guys are with him."

"We are. Here's his number. Contact him if you ever need him or hear anything else about Annie or the Keeper," Striker said as wrote a phone number down and handed it to Petey.

"Will do, man. Hope you find the girl."

"Thanks. We owe you." Striker and Gator waved and left the alley as quiet as they'd arrived.

* * *

Petey learned at an early age not to trust anyone. It only caused him to get the crap beat out of him by his father. That was until he was big enough to defend himself. At fifteen he'd broken his father's nose and a few ribs before high-tailing it out of Manhattan. He'd lived off the streets for two years now.

So, with that thought in mind he followed Striker and Gator at a smart distance. That's when he saw two large shadow's move out from the darkness behind the two boys. Both held what looked like baseball bats. Before Petey could scream out a warning, both bats swung hard and connected to the back of the boy's skulls with a crack. Both boys went down.

Petey watched Striker being thrown over a huge gorilla shaped shoulder. Gator was lifted and thrown over the other guys shoulder. Petey got a look at the second guy's face. It was ugly enough to make him shudder. The goons carried both boys out of the alley. He followed them and watched them throw the boys into the back of a dark SUV. Both boys were unconscious.

Gorilla got into the driver's seat while Horse-face sat in the back with the unconscious teens. Gorilla drove off, keeping at a slow, unsuspicious pace down the narrow streets.

Petey jogged behind them and caught up at the lights when they turned red in his favor. Twelve blocks later, the SUV turned into the parking lot of a large metal warehouse. A large door began rolling up and the vehicle disappeared inside.

Panting for breath, Petey looked around at his surroundings trying to decide what to do. His heart pounded in fear. He wiped his damp palms against his worn jeans and decided to retrace his steps a block back. Thank God this part of town had 24 hour convenience store. Surely it had a phone he could use. He took off at a run. He had to call Teach.

And, then he had to disappear.

*** *

Annie lay back on her bed after the Keeper threw her back into her room. Her jaw ached from the hard slap across her face. She could feel one eye swelling shut.

She bit down on a fist to stifle the sound of her crazy laughter escaping from her split lips. A ray of hope blossomed in her heart for the first time since she'd stupidly left her safe haven with Teach.

Teach and the boys were looking for her. They hadn't given up as she'd feared.

Oh God. They were looking for her.

CHAPTER TWENTY-EIGHT

"I'm telling you, we have no life," Dobbs complained. He glanced at his watch. "It's ten o'clock on a Sunday night and we're still in your office working."

Tara shrugged. "Beats going home to an empty apartment. Jake won't be home from his buying trip until tomorrow night. And, you don't have anyone leaving the home fires burning for you, either. Just think. You have my wonderful company for the next few hours while we go over our notes, one more time."

"I would've enjoyed your company even more if you'd ordered a pizza delivered."

"Is food all you think about?"

Dobbs grinned. "Nope. Food comes in a close second, if you know what I mean." Brows rose up and down.

Tara snorted. "So, if you can't have the first you'll settle for second? Is that what you're saying?"

"Yep. That just about covers it."

Laughter erupted. She loved working with Dobbs. Not only was he pleasant to the eyes, but his sense of humor matched hers. They made a great team. If Jake hadn't been in the picture she might've been tempted to make him forget all about food.

And, she had no doubt she could. He never bothered to hide his appreciation of her rear end. He liked what he saw. But, Jake was an important part of her life, so both she and Dobbs kept their relationship purely professional.

"How about we finish up here and go get a pizza and a beer before heading home?"

She had his attention now.

He sat up straighter. "A pizza and a beer?

"Yep."

"You're on."

Then her phone rang. Wondering who would be calling her office so late, she answered, "Detective Woods."

Melinda's excited voice came over the line. "Thank goodness I caught you before you left for the night. Can you and Dobbs come down to my office right away. I have some great info for you."

"We're on our way." Tara hung up and stood. "That was Melinda. She has something for us."

Taking the stairs down to the third floor, they entered Melinda's domain. High-tech computers lined three walls. Melinda was running from one computer to the next typing on each keyboard. She glanced up as they entered.

"What do you have for us?" Dobbs asked.

Melinda pointed at the computer screen she was standing in front of showing a young man with scraggly long hair and dead eyes. He was dressed in a county orange uniform. "See him? He was convicted two years, ago for grand auto theft. He goes by the name Montana. Evidently, because that's where he was born."

Tara glanced at the boy. "Okay. What's so important about him?"

A wide grin appeared on Melinda's face. "He knows the Teach and knows his real name."

"What? How? Seriously?" Dobbs almost yelled in his excitement.

"Seriously. Like you asked, I put the word out to all of the local jails and penitentiaries around to see if any of the guards had heard any convicts mention the name Teach. I lucked out. This guy here knows who he is. I just got off the phone with Montana and his lawyer. He says he was one of Teach's original students, until he got caught."

Always suspicious, Dobbs asked, "Why is he talking now?"

"Evidently, the Teach was supposed to have bailed him out, but he was a no show. He's since been convicted and sentenced. He'll be in there for a few years. I would say revenge against the Teach for leaving him in there is his high priority right now. He hates Teach's guts."

"I'm sure he's not the only one," Dobbs drawled.

"Which reminds me…," Melinda walked over to another computer and pulled up the large screen showing mug shots of four young teen boys. "Montana turned on these guys, as well. From left to right is Joe Marks, Steve Randall, Mark Jackson and Todd Mason. They are better known on the streets as Striker, Gator, BoneZ and Cruiser. All four have rap sheets a mile long. According to Montana, they're also Teach's students and live with him. They do his dirty work for him from robbing homes to fencing stolen goods. And, guess what else. The DNA found beneath Mr. Chambers' nails matches the DNA of the boy called Gator."

"Holy crap. You're a genius, Melinda. I bow to you," Dobbs told her.

Melinda grinned. "And, don't you forget it."

Tara grinned, as well. "We both owe you big time. What else did you learn?"

"I asked Montana if he'd ever lived with the Teach. He said he hadn't, but he knew the address. Before he'd been caught, he'd overheard a phone conversation one day where Teach was talking to one of his real estate clients and he gave his name. He didn't know Montana was anywhere around." Melinda stopped and grinned big. "Do you want to know who your Teach is?"

"Hell, yea! Tell us."

Melinda gave them the name.

Tara whooped in triumph. "I knew it." Her cell phone began ringing. Still grinning, she answered, "Detective Woods."

"The Keeper has two of my boys. I need your help. He's taken them to a warehouse. Here's the address. Please hurry." The phone went dead.

Tara's grin vanished. She turned to Dobbs. "Let's go. I'll explain later. Thanks for everything, Melinda." She took off running knowing Dobbs was right on her heels.

CHAPTER TWENTY-NINE

The bedroom door flew open startling Annie. Thinking it was another customer entering, she cringed and scooted into a small ball and whimpered. But, instead of a john, two bodies were thrown to the floor. Before the door closed and locked, she saw in the dim light who lay there.

Muffling a cry out, she scooted across her bed and fell to her knees beside the bodies. "Striker? Gator?"

They didn't move or make a sound.

"Oh God, please, please be alive." She knelt over them searching for injuries. Her hands felt the dried, crusty blood on the back of their head and shoulders. Feeling no pulse on their wrists, she placed her cheek against each of their lips checking for a breath, anything to show they lived. When she felt the warm breath caress her cheeks, she cried out in relief. They were both alive.

Barely.

For now.

Rising, she gathered her cold water and the cloth she'd used earlier to take a sponge bath. With extreme care, she washed the blood off trying to locate the wounds with her fingers.

The back of their skulls were both swollen and bloody. But, thankfully the bleeding had stopped. But, they weren't out of the woods, yet. She worried about any other injuries or bleeding occurring inside their bodies that she couldn't detect.

For at least thirty minutes, she dealt with the outside injuries. Kneeling beside them, she took turns with each boy. She held the cold cloth against the swellings on the back of their heads. Exhausted and scared, she cried out in relief when Gator moaned and began thrashing about. He tried to open his eyes, but failed. He groaned and passed out again. She didn't know much about it, but she figured they had a concussion.

She stood and began pounding on the locked door. She needed to get them to the hospital. Now.

Then the door opened. Two men started dragging Annie and the two boys out of the room one at a time.

Annie screamed, frightened of the unknown.

* * *

Teach, BoneZ and Cruiser in their street clothes watched the abandoned warehouse at the address Petey gave them. Within the ten minutes of surveillance, one semi pulling a trailer and one Mercedes had driven through the raised metal door.

Whether Striker, Gator or Annie were inside either the car or the semi, they couldn't tell with the dark, tinted windows and enclosed trailer.

While hidden behind a row of overgrown bushes lining the side of the building, they had a brief glance inside before the sliding door lowered. Several armed men stood around watching the vehicles enter.

Other than the one small door beside the sliding door, Teach could see an exit door in the back. One guy stood next to it with a rifle in his hand, but he moved forward watching the vehicles entering.

Teach tapped the shoulders of his students and motioned toward the exit door in the rear. It was less guarded, but without a doubt locked. That was Cruiser's specialty. He could pick a lock within seconds.

The three ran at a crouch allowing the shrubs to hide them in the darkness. Teach and BoneZ kept watch while Cruiser pulled out his tools and picked the lock. Teach froze as each click sounded like a bullhorn in an acoustic room to his ears. He relaxed when the clicking stopped and Cruiser looked up at him with a cocky grin. He turned the knob and the door creaked open.

Cruiser peeked around the door. Noticing the goon had moved even closer to the activity at the front entrance, he motioned to Teach and BoneZ that all was clear. He stiffened when a loud familiar click sounded behind them.

"Welcome to the party, boys." Two armed men stood behind them. Each packed a pistol and both were aimed at the boys. Searching the three, the men found the boy's handguns and disarmed them.

"The Keeper has been waiting for you." One of the goons, evidently the one Petey had dubbed 'Gorilla' motioned with his gun for the three to proceed them further into the warehouse. Horse face followed close behind the boys hurrying them with his gun barrel in their backs.

Teach, looking around for any type of weapon or chance to escape noticed broken and bent metal shelves lined one wall. Old rusty assembly belts and machinery were pushed into one corner. Several offices with doors hanging off their hinges and others with closed doors lined the other wall.

Sheets of paper and trash was strewn across the concrete floor by either the wind or vagrants living in the building. Large overhead lights brightened the dingy room. The semi was parked in the center of the room with the Mercedes parked beside it. The driver opened his door and stepped outside. He moved to the back and opened the door on his side. A well-dressed man climbed out.

Glancing toward Teach and the boys, a grin emerged on the man's face. Then, he laughed. Big guffaws of laughter doubled him over. Tears rolled down his fat cheeks in mirth. His goons grinned uncomfortably glancing from the Keeper to the Teach.

Stunned, Teach could only stare. He shook his head back and forth. "Un···fuckin'···believable. You? You're The Keeper?"

Still chuckling, The Keeper nodded and bowed. "The one and only. And, I take it that you're the Teach?"

"I am."

The Keeper motioned to his hired goons and they trained their guns on the boys. "I always liked you, boy." He walked up to Teach, his gaze hardened. "But, now you've put your nose into my business and tried to get into a pissing contest with me. I can't let that happen. You took away one of my highest paying income and caused me to lose money." Raising his hand, he slapped Teach across the cheek. "No punk kid like you will ever screw me over."

Teach's head snapped back, but now he stared into The Keeper's eyes. His glacier gaze caused The Keeper to take a step back. Visions of his father's fist hitting his young cheek enraged him.

Teach grinned, his teeth showing like a bear growling. "I'm going to kill you, just like my boys killed your parents. Slow and painful."

The Keeper yelled out in rage. "You bastard. Kill him." He shouted to his men. "Kill him."

A gun barrel smashed against Teach's temple sending him to his knees. A shot rang out, the bullet entered into his shoulder, but it didn't deter him. Teach forced himself to his feet, blood poured from the wound. Dizzy, he growled. "And, no low-life dealing in human flesh will again touch me or what is mine. Where is Annie?"

"That's what we would like to know." Tara and Dobbs slipped through the door with six officers surrounding them, guns drawn. Turning back to one of the officers, she ordered, "Check the trailer and the other rooms. Someone call an ambulance."

Dobbs motioned toward The Keeper's men with his handgun. "Lay your weapons on the floor and move away. Now."

The goons looked toward their boss. When he nodded, they each placed their guns on the floor and stepped back.

"Thank God, you're here, Detectives. Teach and his boys are the ones who killed and robbed my parents. I have the proof you need. He confessed. Arrest them." The Keeper told them.

Tara nodded. She glanced toward Teach who was swaying back and forth on his feet trying to stem the flow of blood with his hand. "Oh, I believe you, Senator Chambers. Regardless of what Teach aka Chase Masters, the real estate mogul, aka Carl Mason, the street kid with a rap sheet a mile long tried to make us believe, we know he's the one who murdered and robbed your parent's. He has a long history of murder and theft, including murdering his own parents. He and his students have turned it into a profitable business. They will have their date with a jury soon. But you Senator Chambers, you are the one who sickens me. Or, should I call you The Keeper? You'll also have your day in court. And, when they try and convict you, I hope you rot in jail and then in hell. Officers, read them their rights and cuff them all."

Senator Chambers grinned, challenging her. "I want a lawyer now. Call my son, Justin and tell him to meet me at the precinct and bring a lawyer from his firm. They'll have me out of there in no time."

"Like I said, Senator, you and slime ball here will have your day in court, no matter how many lawyers your son brings." Tara took the challenge.

Teach growled, his teeth bared. "Don't ever talk down to me, Deee···tec···tive. You are worthless. You would have never captured The Keeper if I hadn't taught you the skills you sorely needed."

Tara grinned. "Oh, believe me. I would have. But, thanks to you calling me with the information of his whereabouts, I've also captured you and your boys."

"Detectives, you've got to see this," One of the officers called out to them from the back of the trailer. Moving quickly, Tara and Dobbs walked to the back of the trailer. The officer helped them to climb inside. With their eyes adjusting to the dark interior, the officer motioned with his hand.

A thin girl knelt beside two boys lying on the bed of the trailer. The girl was badly bruised, disheveled and crying. The two boys were lying on their backs with their eyes open, moaning and in pain.

"Annie?"

With a glazed look, she glanced up at Tara and nodded.

Tara knelt beside her and put an arm around her. "You're safe now, Annie. Let's get you home." She turned back to Dobbs. "We'll need another ambulance."

With a softness soothing his features, Dobbs nodded and pulled out his cell phone. "I'll tell them to hurry."

EPILOGUE

A week later, Tara and Dobbs met with Annie inside the safe house where she would be residing for the next few months. She still had bruises, nightmares and a haunted look in her eyes that would hopefully fade in the future.

She had a long road of recovery ahead of her, but she was a strong survivor. The safe house would provide her with housing, peer and crisis counseling and psychological support which she badly needed. Plus, she had her loving parents who would always be there for her and support her through the hard times ahead with her recovery and upcoming court dates. Tara hoped the lawyers didn't call Annie to testify against Senator Chambers, but it was a strong possibility.

Sitting in the group recreation room, Tara held Annie's hand while they talked. Tara and Dobbs tried to answer all of Annie's questions.

"Teach, BoneZ and Cruiser were released from the hospital and jailed two days ago. Striker and Gator were also arraigned and awaiting trial."

When tears began streaming down Annie's face and a sob escaped, Tara leaned forward and squeezed the girl's hands. "I'm sorry, Annie. I know you were close to them and in a way they were your saviors, but they also murdered a couple and robbed several homes. They have to pay and do time for what they did. It will be up to a jury on how much time they will have to serve. But, on a better note, Senator Chambers' bail was set high at ten million dollars, so he will not be out on bail which is what we wanted. Annie, thanks to your help he will never exploit teens again." Tara looked deep into the girls eyes and smiled. "Never."

* * *

Several hours later, Tara and Dobbs sat in Chief Haynes office. The Chief was in an unusual jubilant mood. "I just got off the phone with Mayor Stavely. He and I are very pleased with the job you two have done to solve this case, or should I say two cases? The Mayor plans on rewarding you for your effort."

Tara smiled. "Thank you, Sir."

"Thank you. And, tell the Mayor thank you, as well. It was just part of our jobs." Dobbs told him. He was never one to sing his own praises.

"Still, it was appreciated. I guess you've noticed the media is having a field day over Senator Chambers' criminal activities and upcoming trial? I believe he's getting more exposure than any other well-known trial cases over the past years." Chief Haynes chuckled. "This may be the one time I appreciate the media."

Tara laughed. "Me too."

"Maybe you should run for the Senate seat since it now has an opening." Dobb told him.

The Chief shrugged. "Maybe. Maybe not. I haven't thought about it. Not much anyway. Now, why don't you two take the weekend off before another case comes up. You deserve some rest and relaxation after these last two weeks."

Dobbs sat up in his chair. "I believe I'll take you up on that, Sir. I know of a large lake full of fish that has been calling my name."

Tara's brow rose. "I never knew you liked to fish?"

"I didn't say I was going to catch the fish. I plan on eating them. Lots of them. But, I do love to fish."

Tara stood shaking her head. "Settling for second choice, again? Lord only knows, we've got to find you a woman."

Connect with JERI LYNN STONE

I really appreciate you reading my books! I
would love to hear from you.
Here are my social media coordinates:

Friend me on Facebook:
http://facebook.com/jerlynstone
Follow me on Twitter:
http://twitter.com/jerlynstone
Subscribe to my blog:
http://www.jerlynstone.blogspot.com
Connect on LinkedIn:
http://www.linkedin.com/in/jerlynstone

If you would like to sign up for my newsletters
email me at jerlynstone@gmail.com.

Watch out for #3 in the 'Tara' Series

Tangle With Tara

The young girls whimpered. Six of them bound with quarter inch thick, heavy chains secured to the wall looked at Detective Tara Woods with blank, tormented eyes. Eyes that had seen the worst kind of hell, a nightmarish hell that would burn in their memories for the rest of their lives.

Tara whispered into the radio to her partner. "Dobbs, get your tail down here. I've found them." She placed her gun into her shoulder holster and beamed her flashlight around the dark and dank basement smelling of feces and stale air. A rat scampered across the dirty floor in front of her and she clamped a hand over her mouth to keep from screaming. Damn, she hated rats almost as much as she hated sick bastards who preyed on young girls.

She heard Detective Dobbs give the "all clear" signal and relaxed. They would lay in wait until the sicko returned. And, she would do everything in her power to make sure he never hurt an innocent, again.